Nat,

Haven't found
any Angell Field
Ancients in Lost
Angles — miss you
guys too much.
Hope to be back
here some day
and run plenty
trails with you.

Best Always

PRAYING FOR RAIN

Praying For Rain

STORIES

CHRIS SPAIN

JOSHUA ODELL EDITIONS CAPRA PRESS 1990

Grateful acknowledgment is made to the publications in which these stories first appeared: "Entrepreneurs" and "Playing Iwo Jima" in *The Quarterly;* "Sounding Underwater" in *Story Quarterly;* "Horizontal Light" and "Let the Babies Keep Their Hearts" (published under the title "Praying for Rain") in *Antioch Review;* "Infant's Big Ache" in *Story.* "Entrepreneurs" was included in *The Pushcart Prize Anthology,* 1988-89.

The author wishes to thank the Colorado State University English Department, the Columbia University Writing Division, the Henfield Foundation, the Stanford University Creative Writing Center, the Squaw Valley Community of Writers, and the Bread Loaf Writers Conference for their generous support. Also special thanks to Eric Ashworth, Miriam Kuznets, Neil Olson, and Joshua Odell.

Published by Joshua Odell Editions, Capra Press
Post Office Box 2068
Santa Barbara, California 93120

LIBRARY OF CONGRESS CATALOGING-IN-PUBLICATION DATA

Spain, Chris, 1956-
    Praying for rain: stories / by Chris Spain
        p. cm.
    ISBN 0-88496-320-9
    I. Title.
PS3569.P336P7   1990   90-6909
813'.54—dc20   CIP

Printed in the United States of America
Design and typography by Jim Cook/Santa Barbara
Author photograph by Catherine Lance Spain

For my Annie-Toot,
and for Jim, Joy, and Catherine.

Thanks to Frank, Grof, and Rock.

Entrepreneurs

Harold reads the musts. He is on must number 4, going backward from 25. Must number 4 is you must get started. Harold reads while I row. I interrupt Harold reading the musts and I say to him, "You know what the last thing they said before they vaporated was?"

"I know," says Harold.

Harold was reading the musts when they vaporated. We were out on *My Toot-Toot*, dragging a sea anchor and barracuda bait and listening to Cocoa Beach Countdown radio, this being the number tenth time we had been out on account of all the times they had called it off. We were wrapped in army surplus and leaning back and drinking 7-Eleven coffees. Harold was on must number 1. Must number 1 is you must develop the ability to see the needs and wants of others. This must had had us stumped for months. It still had us stumped when the water started rattling and we cranked our heads back to watch the thing punch a hole through the sky. When it blew, we were what you might call awed.

"Fourth of July," said Harold.

I said, "I don't think that's what it's supposed to do."

Myrtle keeps her finger, what she calls her "too small a tragedy to keep," in a jar. She holds her hand, the still whole one, dangled over the side into the warmth of the Gulf Stream. At her feet is a burlap bag full of unwanted needs and wants, and seawall stones to drag it down. Harold takes a break from reading the musts. What is left to hear is the sound of oar wood blistering my fingers. I say, "You know what them and Tylenol and a walrus got in common?"

"We know," says Harold.

Our very first thought was honorable. We thought we would motor over there and, if they were still alive, save them. Our very second thought was that with all that machinery dropping out of the sky it would be dangerous to motor over there, and that maybe our very first thought, though honorable, was stupid. Our very third thought was that that thundering shower of tech was a primo example of the needs and wants of others. Stupid or not, we were laying down a wake before the big pieces hit the water.

The twenty-five musts are on the back of *The Start-up Entrepreneur,* a book Harold permanently borrowed from the library on wheels when the librarian was inside the 7-Eleven buying a burrito. On the front of the book it says, "How you can succeed in building your own company into a major enterprise starting from scratch." Harold figured with that information we were halfway to rich already.

Where we are halfway to now is a burial at sea. Harold is reading the musts by flashlight light, while I row by the light of the moon.

"You know why they only sent up one colored, don't ya?" I ask Harold.

"I know," he says.

We got underneath it before the little pieces finished precipitating out of the sky. There was a white cloud still hanging to mark where it had happened. It was feathery like dove dust, what is left on the air when the dove never sees you and you shotgun him point-blank. The little pieces fluttered down on us, and when they hit the water they sounded like belly flop.

Once we cornered must number 1 in our heads, we figured we had must number 2 cold. Must number 2 is you must find a market gap. Our thinking was that the market gap in right-stuff-gone-wrong was about as wide as you could get. We would have a corner on the market of the market gap.

When we found the stain on the water we throttled back to look. We were not prepared for search-and-rescue. We had barracuda poles, a gaffing hook, and a landing net. I hung the net over the side while Harold zigzagged through the ruin of what looked a moon picnic turned loose. It turned out we were floating right on their pantry. The net came back with space food for a week and wet wipes. Harold had a hunger and jumped right on the tubified eggs and was going for seconds when I evoked must number 13 or 14, telling him he was eating our inventory.

While I row, it comes to me that rowing is a strange way to get somewhere, because it puts your back to where you are going. If Columbus had had to row, he probably never would have done it.

"You hear why they're sending the next one up the Fourth of July?" I ask Harold.

"I heard," says Harold.

"You practically invented that one yourself, you co-me-d-ian," I tell him.

We about had the boat full of souvenirs when a chopper whomp-whomped down on us. Leaning out the door was a kid with a kid-looking-for-his-lost-dog look on his face. The bladed air on *my* face took me back so hard that I nearly fell in the water.

"I'm having some kind of violent reaction to that Huey," I told Harold.

"We're here to save you!" megaphoned down the kid.

I was puking over the side already.

"Tell him to go away," I said between pukes.

The chopper settled into its hover.

"Fuck off!" yelled Harold, and he went after the chopper with the gaffing hook.

The kid's face went to ununderstanding.

"But a terrible thing has happened!" yelled the kid.

"It is true," I said.

"Are the rest dead?" asked the kid.

"There is no rest," said Harold.

The kid leaned back in the chopper, and then he leaned back out.

"Are you astronauts?" he asked us.

"Entrepreneurs," said Harold.

The kid looked as if he had just found his dog on the highway, made into motor meat.

I take a break from rowing and say to Harold, "You hear what they had for breakfast?"

"I heard," says Harold.

We were headed for Miller Time with our load of bits and pieces when we saw a school of minnows circling on a floating something. It was a finger. A ring finger with a ring on it.

We netted it and wrapped it in a wet wipe.

■

Must number 7 is you must use the telephone constantly for acquiring all kinds of information. The only phone we had was the pay phone outside our 7-Eleven. Harold, then a believer in all musts, started saving silver.

I asked him, "But who are we going to call?"

"The people with the information," said Harold.

They were waiting for us when we made port. They confiscated everything. We said we were bringing it to them anyway, that we just wanted to help. The Cocoa Beach *Bay Times* ran the story, saying: "Local fishermen help retrieve remains of space heroes." There was a picture of us holding up pieces of bits and pieces—an ambulance had already come to pick up the finger—and they even printed what I said about the fishing, which was that I did not think this terrible tragedy would have too much of an effect on it, that in fact it might make it better, what with all the fish nosing up to see what all the banging was about, and that our boat was available for a scenes-of-the-aftermath charter.

"You hear what they weather-forecasted?" I ask Harold.

"For tonight?" says Harold.

"No," I say. "It's another joke. What they weather-forecasted the morning of."

"I heard," says Harold.

The next day they declared our water off-limits to us and everybody else. They closed the ocean for twenty miles, which is about nineteen miles farther out than we can convince anybody to go on *My Toot-Toot.* We were seriously shored, our economy shot to hell.

Must number 16 is you must develop tenacity and perseverance to survive days and nights of anxiety.

We were halfway through our first night of anxiety, drinking beers and hand-grenading the empties over the side, when we had our collective fourth thought. What we thought was that a wooden boat like *My Toot-Toot*, without the motor, wouldn't show up on their radar screens. What we thought was that we would do some night fishing, junk fishing, casting for the bottom.

Before we got used to being celebrated for saving the only piece of space hero that got saved, they figured out it was no astronaut finger we had fished. It was a finger from a Palm Bay woman. It was Myrtle's, who we didn't know yet. She had come back from work that morning because she wasn't feeling right, and she found her husband doing it with the Twiggy from across the street. Myrtle tried to take her wedding ring off and throw it at them, but her finger was too fat and the ring would not come off. Her husband said to her, "You big ugly thing, can you blame me?"

I say to Harold, "You hear they found that schoolteacher's husband rowing around out here?"
Harold doesn't answer.
"He was rowing around out here just like we are," I say.
Harold still doesn't answer.
"Don't you want to know what he was looking for?" I ask.
"No," says Harold.

In the late afternoons we would wait for the winter dark to come down fast, and then we would unslip *My Toot-Toot* and row her to under where the thing had thundered and stormed itself to pieces. We rigged our poles with speaker magnets that we popped out of Harold's mongo-woofers and dangled them on the deep. It was fishing-booth fishing. We pulled up an ocean full of needs and wants, and a rusty hook with a fish jaw still hanging on.

■

Harold reads must number 26. Must number 26 we made up. Must number 26 is if musts numbers 1 through 25 don't work.

Her husband called her Myrtle Bitch, after Myrtle Beach, South Carolina, where they had driven to for their honeymoon. Myrtle tried dish soap, sewing-machine oil, and WD-40 that she found in the garage. But the ring stayed on. She says she felt as if her whole self were being strangled by that ring. She left the house not knowing where she was headed. She ended up at the docks, so weak from no air in her head that she had to lean on a piling for help. Then she heard the same rattling on the water that we were hearing, and she looked up to watch it soar. For those seconds she forgot the heaviness of her body, and she soared also.

Must number 6 is you must start small. We advertised on telephone poles. Our sign said: OWN HISTORY. *If you witnessed this event, you'll need and want a souvenir to remember your memories with. Grand opening tonight!*
We set up a tent on the beach.

After our ungrand grand opening, Harold decided there had to be a more elemental must that came before must number 1. Now the first must is must number 0, which is that you must hit someone before they hit you. We learned must number 0 the hard way.

When the thing blew, Myrtle lost all the balance she had left. She had a pain in her chest that she said came from deeper than where earthquakes come from, and she thought she might fault open. Beside her on the dock was a kid skipping school so he could watch the men he wanted to be sky their machine. He had been scaling a little bait fish, but now his jaw was hanging unhinged and his scaling knife was hanging in his hand. Myrtle grabbed his knife, put her ring finger to the wooden piling, put the knife to the ring finger, and good-bye ring and finger.

The day after we heard the news that we weren't heroes anymore for saving the only piece of space hero that got saved, a sheriff came by to tell us that by marine salvage law the ring was ours. He said he would have to give the finger back to Myrtle. We told him to give the ring back to her, too.

Myrtle left a message at the 7-Eleven that she wanted us to come to St. Luke's to see her. We bought a flower. They had her strapped down. The finger, which was hers, and the ring, which by marine salvage law was ours, were in a specimen jar on the nightstand. She thanked us for saving the finger, and then she said she wanted us to throw it back.

"Back where?" we asked.

"If the fish is too small, you throw it back, don't you?" said Myrtle.

We said that was mostly true.

"Just think of it as too small a tragedy to keep," she said. "And throw it back."

We left her leaning hard on her straps so as to smell the flower.

Our grand opening turned out not to be. They called us frauds and said that what we had was nothing but dumpster trash. Then they turned patriot on us, said we were disrespectful, defiling the dead, et cetera, and that this was no joke. I asked them if they had heard the walrus and Tylenol one. Harold asided to me that the mood of America in general and this crowd in particular would make it difficult for them to appreciate the punch line.

He was right.

I stop rowing when we are under where it all rained down.

Myrtle said she wanted her finger buried with all the rest of the truth. The truth is, we do not know how to do a burial at sea. We drop the seawall stones in the bag full of unwanted needs and wants, Myrtle's finger, too, and let it go.

"What do we say?" says Harold.

"I've never done this," I say.

Myrtle doesn't know, either. Above us, astronaut footprints all over her face, is the moon.

Failed entrepreneurs, Harold and I sat on a driftwood to do our where-did-we-go-wrong thinking. When we finally saw it through our raccooned-by-patriot eyes, we saw it so clear that it knocked us to the sand. What we saw was that we had identified the needs and wants all wrong. What people want is to see other people get blown to shit. What they need is to see what dead looks like. It makes them feel more here, seeing others not here.

We tested our new understanding of needs and wants on the four-way stoplight in front of the 7-Eleven. It didn't take any time at all. A red Chevy slammed an old Ford pickup, then a Volvo piled on. The local television and both newspapers sent people. But when they discovered that the signal box had been rewired for go-green all the way around, it made the Miami news. The announcers shook their heads and said, Who could be so coldhearted, and how lucky because it could have been a school bus full of children. They did not say it would have made a better story if it had been a school bus full of children.

We went back to St. Luke's to pick up Myrtle's finger. We were throwing everything else back, we figured why not that, too. We couldn't leave her. We asked her if she wanted a career of giving people what they needed, what they wanted. It made perfect sense to Myrtle.

■

I turn my back on accident, tragedy, mayhem, and disaster, and lean into the oars. We are off to give you what you need and want, what you are looking for.

"You know what the last thing they said before they vaporated was?" I ask Harold.

"I already said I knew," says Harold.

"I mean for real," I say.

"You mean on the recording?" asks Harold.

"After that," I tell him.

"Would you look at this," says Myrtle.

We look at Myrtle.

"That's the last thing they said," she says.

Infant's Big Ache

INFANT SITS AT THE END of the pier of the Admiral on the
Beach Hotel, Galveston, Texas. It is the last day of
December and does not seem right. The humidity of this
place in winter is not right. It's something Infant hasn't
known since he and Kid Billy sailed into the Big Heat, the
Big Heat that was World War Two. The heat and humidity
take him back. Humidity that lies on his lungs, choking
him on tiny teaspoonfuls of air, as if he is getting old. And
he is getting old. A sea gull wheels across the wide open and
welcoming sky and dives and Infant thinks, Sea gull, if I
could fly like you.

Infant and Kid Billy sailed into the Big Heat on an aircraft carrier called Our Fat Lady. Kid Billy handed Infant
the flags. That was their job; flag-talking with the rest of the
flock. They were what the Captain called his last line of
communication. Number three behind the finger-chattering
radio operator and the semaphore flasher who spoke with

smokey lamps. But the Captain would come down from his bridge and say, Practice, practice, if we lose our electricity, if our lamps crack, you will be our voice, you will be our ears. So they flag-talked silly jokes across the water. They asked the other flag-talkers what one knee said to the other knee. They made up signals not in *A Sailor's Reader*. They drew on the air what they wanted to do to each other's sister, to each other's mother, to every geisha girl in Yokohama too.

When Infant and Kid Billy first saw Our Fat Lady, their hoes just three months dropped in an August cotton patch, she was leaning against a dock, the ocean she was floating on the first ocean they had ever seen. Our Fat Lady was leaning hard because she had taken big lamb-slaughter hits. Infant and Kid Billy scampered up the gangway and tumbled on to the deck. The old salts, who called themselves Sea Daddies, looked up from what they were doing, which was cleaning war from Our Fat Lady, and they laughed. They said, Look what, more lambs for the slaughter. They said, Oh no, somebody has started robbing nurseries, here's almost a kid, and practically an infant, too.

The Sea Daddies gave Infant and Kid Billy the don't-fall-off-the-boat tour. They said, The first and most important and only thing to always remember is to never fall off the boat. They said, Our Fat Lady takes three miles to stop. There was the foot line to tell you you were close to the edge, there was the housing line to tell you you were too close to the edge, there was the life line, which was something to grab on to, there was the Save-All, to catch you if you missed grabbing on, and if you missed everything, there was a thousand yards of Jesus line dragging in Our Fat Lady's wake. But you had to swim fast. The don't-fall-off-the-boat tour over, the Sea Daddies put Infant and Kid Billy to cleaning corners, where Infant found a crusted war driblet, and he said to himself, Already I am no infant.

■

Tanker waves beat the pier pilings at Infant's feet, slap, slap, right up to the shore; butterflies drumming glass killing jars, stubborn in their stubborn deaths, ruining their wings for mounting. Infant watches the water as if he's still waiting for Kid Billy to come up for air. This is really no ocean, thinks Infant, It's just a big mud thing. If only they could see. If only they could see what I saw, such beautiful water it was, so wide and blue, so blue and clear, so clear and dangerous.

Infant had just signaled the one about Tojo's little dick, the one about Tokyo Rose saying, Is it in yet? He was waiting for a chortle of flag-laughter to cross the water when the Emperor's nimble and gallant death pilots crossed the dog-watch picket instead, and swarmed for Our Fat Lady in the middle. When the yolk of the first bomb washed up against the radio room, exploding the radio boy's chat-chat fingers, peeling banana skins back from his bones, when it blew the semaphore flasher right through his lights, Infant said to Kid Billy, Give me X, and he told the startled flock, Stop carrying out your intentions and watch my signals. When the bombs struck with such force that the bridge was cleaved open, meat-lockered, Infant said, Kid Billy, give me D, and told them, Keep clear, I'm maneuvering with difficulty. When the explosions put Kid Billy over the side, over the foot line, over the housing line, over the life line, over the Save-All, Infant said, Kid Billy, give me O, we have a man overboard. But Kid Billy had gone over with O.

Infant drools because he took heavy damage behind the eyes. He still thinks it's some funny joke that he made it through the Big Heat without a scratch, that he made it through that and husband and farmer and father and grandfather and then he was putting a fork of scrambled eggs into his mouth when a blood vessel blew. Infant went, Damage control, he went, Keep clear of me I'm maneuvering with difficulty, he went, Stop carrying out your intentions and watch my signals, he went down hard. That was how Alanna found him, hard on the linoleum with scrambled eggs on his face. Now he travels in his polished chair, drools, but understands fine. He thinks, Oh, Kid Billy, you missed so much, oh, you missed so much.

When the Big Heat was finished and Infant went home, he looked the same but could no longer plow a straight line. He sat on the roof of the tractor shed and signaled one-sided conversations to the broad sides of barns. He signaled, I cannot use my radio due to sickness of the operator. He signaled, Death, by, from . . . He signaled, These signals are not intended for you. He signaled, I am sinking, send boat to take off crew. He spent days and nights drawing Kid Billy's favorite jokes on the West Texas sky, and then he laughed his own ho, ho, ho's until he fell over.

After a fall and a winter and most of a spring, Infant climbed down off the roof of the tractor shed for good. He wrapped his flags in a Sunday *Avalanche Journal* and put them into a cardboard box which he pushed deep into the shelter closet. He walked back to the tractor shed, tugged open the floor-to-ceiling wooden doors, climbed up on the Case that was resting inside, and pressed the starter. He plowed a fallow field north to south and then east to west, just to be sure he could. He went to a social at the Methodist Church. He stood next to a wall with a Coca-Cola in his hand. A girl named Alanna walked over to him. Her mother had just said, That's the Carpenter boy, go say hello. She said, Hello, I'm Alanna.

It seems like no New Year's Eve to Infant. The children play on the beach. They make brutal childrens' noises. They run up the pier, stand too close to the edge. The first and most important and only thing to always remember is to never fall off the boat. They buzz around him, sand flies he would swat if he could. The children say, Grandfather, help us fly our kite. He signals, Keep clear of me. The children fly their kite in the wide open and welcoming sky, shouting, Watch, watch, watch. Infant thinks, They are what you leave behind, when you take the final plunge, they are the flotsam.

Sometimes Infant forgot about Kid Billy for all of half a day. He might have breakfast with Alanna, drive to town, drop a tire at Johnny's Sinclair, have a coffee at the Tasty Freeze, talk to Wallace, Vic, and the Mexican, eat lunch, cultivate half a field of cotton, and then he would be throwing an armload of siphons into the back of his pickup, or he would be standing on the front wheel of the old Case, filling it full of fuel, or he would be on top of the windmill platform, tightening down a blade, or he would be listening to the gas hiss through the above-ground main out by the mailbox on the road, or he would be in the middle of a field unhooking a piece of machinery from the ball hitch on his pickup, or he would be wiping mud from the bottoms of his boots, or he would be out in the shelter, leaning into the floor freezer, reaching for something Alanna put up in summer, or he would be standing next to Alanna, his arms out in front of him to gather in the blindingly white sheets she unpinned from the drying line, or he would be feeding the barn cats, calling to them, Miss, miss, miss, and he would remember Kid Billy's barefoot kicking feet, and the splash they made.

A refinery haze hangs over Galveston Bay. The sun fights the mud-slop ocean, loses, and disappears. Texas City cracking towers jump out on the dark like just plugged in Christmas trees, and the burn of the flare gas could be ships sinking forty or fifty years ago. Lights from boats heading up the ship channel speak a language Infant no longer understands. He waits for his night eyes. They come almost useless now. On the deep ceiling he can only see the very brightest ones, the Hunter's Belt, the Dog Star. Sparklers. The brutal children whirl sparklers that spark and tinkle on the night air and then arc to the water, to tish and expire.

Infant has a memory of sitting with Kid Billy, hanging their feet over the side of Our Fat Lady, the hemp and tar of the Save-All the only thing between their toes and deep nothing, watching the farewell buoy disappear over the horizon. He remembers Kid Billy taking off his ring, putting it in the L of his elbow, squeezing his biceps and saying, This is what it feels like. It's soft like this, and right there, in the pink crack, there's no hair. Infant looked over the stern, watched the farewell buoy disappear, and he thought, I'm going to die without ever tasting it. He took Kid Billy's ring and hid himself in the darkness at the bottom of the big ship, with the ring in his elbow, feeling it and then pulling on his baby-self, trying to imagine, pulling until he almost broke himself off.

When the death pilots in their Zeros and Kates made the dog-watch picket without a loss, it was scramble in the air time. But Our Fat Lady's hunters were on a safari of their own. Only the cripples had stayed, sickly machines that muttered and struggled for altitude as the red sunned ships swept in with pulsing engine exhausts. The Emperor's boys smeared Our Fat Lady's boys across the sky's canopy, two-blink phosphors streaking the glass.

When Infant saw Kid Billy's feet flop on the water and disappear, his first thought was that the Save-All didn't save Kid Billy. He yelled, Swim, Kid Billy, swim, swim fast for the Jesus line. But there was no one there to hear. The water stayed smoothed over. Then Infant thought, At least Kid

Billy tasted it before he took the Big Trip. Infant stood to watch the death pilots make their water-walking splashes. He didn't duck behind any splinter screen. He looked up and said, Look at me, I'm taking the Big Trip before I ever tasted it. But it wasn't true. Infant didn't take the Big Trip, and when they made port he tasted it. He tasted it until he could finally lay back and lick his lips and say, Okay, okay now, I'm still afraid, but now it's okay.

Our Fat Lady stopped on the water. She was cracked open by so many bombs laid upon her. The ocean crept up from both ends until her middle couldn't hold anymore and she hog-backed. Infant issued frantic blurts of flag cries. Haste-haste, danger-danger, this vessel in a sinking state. Water slapped at Infant's ankles. His flags floated at his waist, the cloth hanging thick, sticking to his arms, garbling his messages; Torpedoes broken sink, Big pussy shit, Dead crack dead. With water at his neck Infant went to signal Sierra Oscar Sierra to the flock. But the O of Oscar was the O of man overboard, and it had already made that trip clutched in the hands of Kid Billy, who by then must have been tucked into a seaweed bed on the ocean bottom.

A sea gull wheels on the dark and dives, flies straight into the glass window of Infant's heart. It beats its wings on his chest. This is an ache. A thud, thud, thud that won't go away. Infant pulls himself up from his chair, stands, and shakes his head. He staggers to the end of the pier, stares hard at the beautiful blue water. But there. What's that there? Infant paws his shoes off, crawls under the railing. Right there. Splash. Kid Billy? Splash, splash, splash, splash. Kid Billy? This water is cold. The first and most important and only thing to always remember. What was it? Splash, splash, splash. Oh. Infant signals, Give me O, we have a man overboard. He signals, Stop carrying out your intentions and watch my signals. Then he says to himself,

Who are you talking to? Splash. Splash. Is this the Big Trip? Kid Billy? Splash. Infant looks up into the wide open and welcoming sky, and thinks, If anyone is going to throw down a Jesus line it had better be now.

Katie Pushing
Back the Dark

KENSINGTON FREE TIME. A basketball pings off cement. Katie, in deep grass out of the drag-mower's reach, leans back against a downed light pole that is pale as fallen soldiers, broken in the middle, rebar showing like open bone, rust staining the concrete like old blood. Katie leans back on white skin elbows. The rest of her is tan, except the ankle-burn memory of a motorcycle crashed in summer.

I'm on this hill watching the sun go down, thinks Katie. That's who I am for sure.

A long Farmer Will shadow, a long Dread shadow, and two long horse shadows cross the cricket pitch. The horses throwing the shadows, called Boy and Horse, lay their hooves forward and out as if they are laying out upside-down coffee cups on a dirt counter. Farmer Will jumps down from Boy, kicks up two red dirt storms, lifts the corral gate hitch, swings the gate open, and, tugging horses, disappears into the shadowed space beneath the overhang of the horse barn roof. There is the sound of saddles dropping, the jangle of bits worked from the horses' mouths, and the metal on wood of bit and rein hung from nails on the horse barn wall.

Katie watches the new kid, his arms stretched wide, gallop his feet across the almost horizontal light that still works itself through the mesquites and grasses. He's so skinny his hip bones show through the khakis cinched to his waist. He runs with his eyes closed, lifting his knees high, his face leaning into the wind. When he reaches the cement of the runway he just keeps on going, all the way to where he loops Snugglebunny, the old crash-landed B-17, and then he climbs the hill and does it all over again. Another Kensington crazy, thinks Katie. Where does old Pitney keep dreaming them up?

That South American dirt-eater Farmer Will has planted himself in his garden. He bends over the earth, pawing at it, lifting it to his mouth. The Dread separates herself from the horse-barn shadow and crosses the orange tile bridge over the empty creek bed, her own shadow reaching and then bending up short on the hillside bottom. Dark eyes, dark hair, dark skin. She picks her way along the footpath as if she were walking across a field of flowers. High cheeks you can almost see bones through. She reaches the top of Katie's hill.

"What are we doing?" asks The Dread.

"Watching this new crazy," says Katie.

The new kid races across the basketball court, dodging traffic, his arms still trying to be wings.

"Hey," shouts a basketballer.

"Thinks he's a plane," Katie says.

The Dread sits on the crumbled concrete.

"Who is he?" asks The Dread.

"Must've gotten thrown out of somewhere," says Katie. "Getting here October already."

■

Pilot, he flies. Across the big blue stretched tight from red dirt to red dirt. Across so much flying weather. He doesn't yet believe what he's seeing. A real goddamn runway. A real goddamn B-17. How come he never heard of this place? He should have been here all his life. Rudder out left over the wide open green space, cross the empty creek bed, shadow shadowing the red dirt and scraggly mesquite below. Sixteen point barrel roll across the picture perfect, holding each point just too long, until he stone drops out of the sky, down to the prairie flat, screaming. Gather it, gather it, stick back to make the hill. Two girls.

"What's your excuse," says the all arms and legs one.

The sun is on its knees, a lost kickball in the far end of the playing field grass, but still pulling out those greens. Dexter once told Katie that late afternoon light was the hands down best light because it came in sideways, air-filtered, having to work its way through the same as fifteen overhead skies all laid out in a row.

"Some colors," says The Dread.

"Makes you happy to be alive," says Katie. "Even if you're not."

"Me too," The Dread says.

"Let's eat," says The Dread.

"I'm watching this sun go down," says Katie.

The Dread hits at her jeaned knees, knocking dirt from them, and then she walks across the dirt and grass saddle between the edge of Katie's hill and the cafeteria.

Farmer Will hunkers to his earth, kneading it, old corn stalk shadows washing over him. When the new kid screams past, Will ducks into his pumpkins, the perfect camouflage for his big head and brillo pad of orange-red hair. Farmer Will thinks in a confusion of Spanish and English and pictures, but if it were all translated into English, what he is thinking now is: That guy's a plane. He can fly. Look at him, flying all the way to there, to the other side of the cement, to almost where I can't see him. I can fly like that if I want. That's nothing. Now he's coming back. Here he comes, he's throwing bombs at me, son of a bitch, he's going to get me with his bombs, he's a war plane, I'm an anti-plane gun. Boom! Boom! Boom!

The sun is knocked down. It gets behind the horse barn, the water tower, the fences, and Farmer Will, leaving purple spaces of shadows, and then it gets so low that the shadows puddle in the shallows of the grass, and the puddles leak over into each other. The earth falls in on itself. The far grain silos of Crockett leave first, then the mesquites on the prairie, and then the prairie too.

Katie throws a clod at Will to let him know it's time to eat. He stands up from his pumpkins. The new kid is still on the runway, his silhouette running across the scattered leftovers of sunset, still trying to get into the air. Katie puts two fingers to her mouth and whistles, but he doesn't seem to hear.

Pilot is caught looking in a different direction when the sun completely hangars itself in the far distance of New Mexico, dropping out of day sky, slamming big night doors down on him.

"Hey," says Pilot, suddenly zooming along through the dark.

He chops down his throttles, tries to get back in touch with the ground. Slowing on the big space of concrete runway, Pilot stumbles over rows of grass-sprouting tar creases. Finally at a stop, he sways, unsure of which way to turn. Above his head stars are already knocking holes through the blue-black blanket. He doesn't look up. Light that is millions of years old and just getting here hammerhead stalls him, sends him spinning for the ground. Pilot kneels to the cement for balance. He feels the warmth of the gone sun that the cement still holds. He holds himself with his arms.

"Hang on, you," says Pilot.

Katie and Farmer Will make their way through the cafeteria to Dexter's table. Dexter is already eating, so is The Dread.

"Katie," says Dexter. "How you been?"

"Me, I'm not complaining," says Katie.

"How about the Farmer?" asks Dexter.

Farmer Will almost nods his head off, grinning.

"You?" says Katie to Dexter.

"Me?" says Dexter. "Me? I've been practicing the pole vault all day. Going out for the Olympics."

They don't laugh. Dexter is in a wheelchair. Ever since he painted what he calls his burning-brick-from-three-thousand-feet self-portrait, which also broke his back.

"That was a joke," says Dexter. "Ho, ho, ho."

"Ho, ho, ho," says Katie. "Dexter is a very funny guy."

"I am," says Dexter. "Aren't I?"

At Dexter's table they have finished eating and are listening to a Dexter story when Neville Pitney hurries into the room. He waves his hands in the air but Katie can't make out what his high pitched voice is saying. He rushes from table to table.

"Dessert with us, Neville?" says Dexter.

Even when he's not talking Neville Pitney's jaw won't rest. He works it up and down.

"Our new student is missing," says Neville Pitney. "Have you seen him?"

"The new senior boy," Neville Pitney says. "Nick is his name."

"I don't think I've even met him," says Dexter.

Neville Pitney grimaces and rushes on.

"He's a senior?" says Katie. "He doesn't look like a senior."

Dexter looks at Katie.

"You know where he is?" asks Dexter.

"He's okay?" Dexter asks.

"Out on the runway," says Katie.

"Doesn't he know it's time to eat?"

"I whistled," says Katie.

"And?" says Dexter.

"I think he's being a plane," says Katie.

"An aero-plane?"

"That's what it looked like."

The path to the hilltop is illuminated by pink halogen street lamps. Dexter calls them nighttime flamingos. The pier of lights stretches to the edge of Katie's hill where the last light pole, Katie's light pole, lies dark on its side. Dexter and Katie and Farmer Will skirt the tall grass and broken cement, then drop into the dark. Katie walks barefoot, sliding down her hill, feeling ahead for the path with her toes. She tries to stay up with Farmer Will but he charges through the dark as if it were daylight. Dexter is tilted back on his back wheels, dropping into the same dark as Katie and Farmer Will, braking himself with his hands, feeling as if he is repelling down the side of a mountain.

"If I lose it," says Dexter. "Scrape me off the bottom."

When Farmer Will reaches the creek bank, he dips down to it, digging dirt chunks from the broken edges. Katie doesn't bother with the bridge but walks the dry bed, running the sand over the tops of her toes. The damp of the cricket pitch brushes scar-high on Katie's ankles. That same dampness wets Dexter's hands as he pushes beside her. They cross the grass, hearing only their drumming hearts, and the crush-crush of the grass beneath them.

This wide lake of darkness throws Dexter back hard to a lot of years ago, looking down, waiting for some heat to show, waiting for a target to acquire. He's plowing through the grease, wading the palms and paddies and thick. He sees some heat and starts circling. He doesn't know it yet but they've laid themselves out on the four points of a cross. He's just reaching for his guns when the supersonic fireflies are unjarred, zooming up to him. They thread the wings, punch them out like sheet metal, fold the machine in half, crucify him, so there is nothing for Dexter to do but hang on and try to give the tattered metal some flying angle other than straight down.

"Can't see much," says Katie.

No real time has passed.

"Un-huh," says Dexter, sounding almost as far away as he is.

Katie opens her eyes wide, trying to let in all the little light there is. She still can't get more than the dark silhouette of earth against the lighter darkness of the sky. She feels a warmth on her skin; it's heat coming up off the concrete of the runway. She steps into it, wraps herself with it, warming the bottoms of her feet and toes.

"Here's the runway," says Katie.

Dexter, stalling bone-jarring hard into memory, jerks himself back, fighting years, pulling out of this old mind picture before he scatters himself on the ground.

You're on an old Air Force runway in Texas, says Dexter to himself. You're with Katie, looking for some lost kid, twenty years from all of that.

Farmer Will won't go out on the cement. It's too big a space of no dirt. He sits down on the grass-frayed edges.

"No?" says Katie.

"Okay," says Katie. "We'll find you on the way back."

The pale slabs of concrete are outlined in grids of once black-tarred now grassed-in creases. Katie kneels every second gap to peer across the cement.

"It's five miles walking fields to Crockett," says Katie. "Plus fences and he doesn't know his way. He wouldn't do that."

Dexter has dragged himself back to Texas. Back to pushing this old wheelchair, heavy on the ground.

"Maybe he just took off," says Dexter.

Pilot searches for what he's hearing. In his head he's all action and direction. Altitude Pilot, you need altitude, you can't do anything here on the ground. Then he sees the two dark on light silhouettes, not twenty feet away, still coming closer, and he freezes.

Dexter has the night eyes, he sees the kid hugging the pavement.

"I see him," says Dexter.

Katie leans into Dexter, to know which way he's looking. The cotton sleeve of her shirt brushes him.

"Where?" says Katie.

Dexter breathes in the smell of Katie; a smell of earth, of dark, thickening. He waits to feel the touch of her hand.

"Two o'clock," says Dexter.

"Between two and three," Dexter says.

Katie sees the kid. He's absolutely still, like a prairie dog frozen at the edge of his hole, listening for something to run from. She walks closer, pushing the dark forward with the skin on her face.

Dexter tries to understand what he's feeling for this girl. This Katie that is so close to a girl he once knew before. She's seventeen, thinks Dexter, and he follows her.

"Tuffffff, tuffffff," says Pilot, firing two Sidewinders.

They take no hits. They're still closing. All you've got left is cannon.

"Braap, braap," says Pilot. "Braap, braap, braap."

They keep coming.

"Oh," says Pilot.

Blow the canopy, hit the silk, take your chances.

■

"He said something," whispers Katie.

"Braap, braap," says Dexter. "I think."

They stop ten feet from the crouching kid. They wait and watch but he doesn't move.

Finally, still in a whisper, thinking that anything louder will knock him over, Katie says, "They're looking for you."

Pilot stands up slowly to face them, swaying, his arms hanging straight down at his sides. In this dark, silhouetted against the pale canvas of the runway, he almost looks as thin as the grassed-in tar creases that frame him.

"You're Nick?" asks Katie.

"Mr. Pitney's looking for you," says Katie. "And probably everybody else too."

"I'm Katie," Katie says.

It's the girl from the hill. Pilot listens to the breathing. And someone else. Who else?

"What are you doing out here?" asks Katie.

Pilot keeps swaying.

"I got lost," he finally says.

"We missed you at dinner," says Dexter. "We thought maybe you didn't know it was dinner time."

That's a teacher, at least, thinks Pilot.

"Why don't you come back with us and get something to eat?" says Dexter.

"I can't see," says Pilot. "I can't see where to go."

"It's over there," Katie says, pointing and then realizing that the kid can't see where she's pointing. "Where the light is past the top of the hill."

Pilot turns his head in the direction he thinks the girl is pointing. Up off the flat, just above the dark line of a hilltop, he sees the pink glow of the street lamps.

"That light?" asks Pilot.

"Yes," says Katie.

"How do I get there?" asks Pilot.

"You can follow us," Dexter says.

Dexter spins his chair and starts wheeling across the runway. Katie walks beside him. Pilot doesn't move.

"I'm Pilot," says Pilot.

Katie, her hand reaching to touch Dexter's shoulder, turns back toward Pilot. Her hand easy on his shoulder. Dexter almost reaches to cover it with his own hand.

"You coming?" Katie asks.

Pilot doesn't move.

Katie leans into Dexter.

"This kid's a mess," whispers Katie.

A wet dirt smell and almost a hurricane in Dexter's head. It unbalances him, leaves him reaching for his rims.

"What do we do?" Katie whispers.

Dexter spins his chair around, feeling as if he is saving himself from something he doesn't want to save himself from, and he wheels over to where Pilot sways.

" Pilot," says Dexter. "You push my chair."

Katie blinks back the dark to watch. She has never seen this before. Just about the first rule any kid learns when they get to Kensington is that you don't touch the guy's chair, ever.

Pilot moves toward Dexter, reaching with his hands, keeping his feet close to the cement.

"The handles," says Dexter.

Pilot gets the handles in his hands.

"Now push," says Dexter.

They start across the runway, Pilot more holding than pushing, Katie walking beside.

"And we have to remember not to forget Will," says Katie.

Sounding Underwater

THE FIRST THING WE THOUGHT when we saw that TV show was that anyone fishing with dynamite *ought* to die of diseases they had no immunities for. Then we thought about those living trophy fish, swimming smart-ass un-caught by us, and there was nothing we could do to save ourselves. They had to die. If someone had told us then that we would have to kill ourselves to kill those fish, we would have jumped gladly into a grave.

Jump into a grave is what we did. Punky stayed. Frank and I crawled from it, having seen it close up. It was the last thing Frank saw. His eyes were sandblasted to the nerve. I was looking, but looking the other way. My eardrums though, they were sheet-on-a-line shotgunned-in-the-breeze. The last thing I ever heard was I heard myself say, "We're going to depth charge the bastards, war at sea."

■

What I think I'm not hearing now is wood on wood. But if a tree falls in the forest with only a deaf man to hear, who is to say? I watch Frank lift the paddle, drip water on water, and then lay it at his feet. He holds the gunnels with both hands, not moving until the canoe stops on the water. He's listening for it to sound the same on all sides. The lake gives the sky a good look at itself. Frank reaches for the casting rod I fixed for him and flies a lure. When it has the distance he wants, he drops it like a duck shot both barrels. It splashes, blurring the sky. I wait for Frank to bring it in. He doesn't. He's casting deep, going for the redwoods, going for General Grant on the bottom.

It turned out we had plenty of dynamite. We packed it in a Saltine can full of sand. The sand was my idea. I said if we didn't pack the dynamite in something we wouldn't get any kind of concussion. What happened was the wires got tangled and I grabbed a fistful and yanked. The copper must have touched. Punky was in front of me. He caught most of what there was to catch. A metal piece that was Saltine can stuck in his chest. He was dripping all over. Frank stumbled for the shore with his hands out in front of him, as if he were playing murder in the dark in the light.

The taking us to see the redwoods might have been a last-ditch effort to save us, but it was only after seeing the redwoods that we could put a name on what we were after. We saw General Grant, Abraham Lincoln, and Auto Log, and we were fine until the ranger showed us General Sherman, the biggest and oldest living thing. He said it was a thousand years older than Jesus Christ; that it would live a thousand years longer than we would. That fact, that it would live a thousand years longer than we would, insulted us more than the smart-ass uncaught fish insulted us. When the ranger turned his back we unpocketed our pocketknives and we were on that tree like lumberjacks.

■

It was the redwoods on the bottom that had us up before the sun, hoping we would suprise them stupid-hungry so that for just one second they would forget how old and wise they were and we could jerk them from the lake. When the man who was our father took us to the hatchery, and we actually saw them, we completely lost our minds. Past any good for breeding, they looked like logs rolling on the water. The hatchery guy said they were his living trophy fish. His. It made us crazy. We couldn't sleep. We called them redwoods, we called them ours, we called them dead. The next morning we didn't even care to throw a line in the lake. And when we did and a little perch latched on, we stomped him into the bank with no pity just because he had occupied our hook.

We had a cabin on the lake then. The porch of that cabin is where I'm sitting now. It's late fall and I think that all the leaves that will fall have fallen, and I'm seeing how close things are that I remembered as far away. Far away is how I remembered everything here, but I don't know if I would go by me if I were you. This is someone who couldn't tell his brother what blue looks like. It makes me think that hearing must have more to do with than just hearing, because it seems to me that more than that is gone. Frank says it still smells the same. What's different to me I'm not sure. All I know is that it's bigger than no wood on wood, no water on water. In the almost dark, Frank's life vest reflects the last orange light in the sky.

It was in no light at all that we fished that summer. We waited until they closed our door, counted until we couldn't, and then dropped into the dark. Our rods and tackle were on the porch. "So we can get an early start," we told them. We walked through the woods and, fishing poles first, rolled under the bottom strand of barbed wire sur-

39

rounding the hatchery. The moisture on the grass, what we called frog piss, brushed our faces. We went straight for where the guy kept the redwoods, his living trophy fish. Frank had us convinced that they would hit so hard they would drag us in. Punky belted himself to me just in case. But it was like throwing rocks at a puddle. We tried everything on a hook. We tried spoons and came back with a fly. We casted ourselves silly in the dark, but we never got a nibble the whole long summer, not one bite.

We called Punky Punky because he was that small. Small enough to slide through the gap beneath the door of the tin shed where they kept the avalanche dynamite. Dynamite they used in winter to bring down big snows in the canyon.

It's dark now and I'm worrying about Frank falling in. What he said before I pushed him away from shore was, "Point me for the middle, I'm going after General Grant." I asked Frank how he would find his way on the lake, and he said that he could tell by listening to the wind on the trees. When he got it so it sounded the same on all sides, he would know he was in the middle. I'm waiting for him to light a match. Then I'll bang an oar on the dock so he can hear his way back.

By the time we were ready to depth-charge the bastards there was light enough to see. It was the kind of light that the man who was our father said on North Atlantic convoy they called the see-who-made-it-through-the-night light. Frank wanted to wait for another night when it was still dark. But I could taste the slaughter already, I could see the beauty of it. The redwoods were awake, log-rolling on the surface, eating breakfast off the water. I said, "Enjoy your last meal, Kraut bastards."

I'm forgetting how to talk. This is what Frank tells me.

He says soon no one will understand. At first he said I sounded as if I were underwater. Now he says I sound as if both of us are underwater. He doesn't actually say, he writes. He wants me to take lessons. He says there are schools for that. Schools that keep you from forgetting. I say to him it's okay as long as he understands.

By the August of that summer we were in a blue fishing funk. That the redwoods would go uncaught was unbearable to us. It made us so weak and skinny in the mirror that we could no longer look at ourselves. We stopped eating and our mother thought we had discovered some evil something that was taking our appetites away. She began to leave our bedroom door open. We had to count until we couldn't twice or three times before we could drop into the dark. In the mornings we could barely climb from our beds. We only had strength enough to lay inside, not talking, staring at a television with sorrowful come-home-empty-handed faces.

The dynamite-raft was a life preserver we ripped from a tree where it was kept to save drowning people drowning in the Swimming Only. We fixed a wire sling in the middle of it, like a hammock, and we hung the Saltine can full of dynamite there. We did "odds or evens" to see who would push it out on to the pond. Punky lost. But in the end Frank and I couldn't keep ourselves from the water. Punky was belly-deep when the wires got tangled. I turned and saw that they were tangled, and I yanked.

I see a flame on the lake. It burns straight up. I walk out on to the dock. The dock is wooden and floats on fifty-five gallon oil drums. It gives beneath my feet and I feel as if this is Look Out, and I'm on a maybe-it-will-maybe-it-won't branch. Punky, who almost weighed nothing, always won at Look Out. The winner was the one who climbed the highest and saw the farthest. To keep going you had to trust the branch, or not care. When the branch broke everyone on the ground looking up would say, "Look out!"

I pound the oar on the dock wood until my arms ache. I don't see Frank until the bow of the canoe thumps in. I light a match to look into the bottom of the boat to see if he caught General Grant, but there's nothing there, except the casting rod, and a hopeless tangle of twenty-pound test wrapped around a red and white Mepps.

Frank has told me that he's forgetting also. He wonders to me if there's a school that could keep him from forgetting what blue looks like. I've tried to tell him what blue looks like, but, finally, I haven't been able to, and I've told him that for myself seeing has been no great help.

It was a program about the Amazon. Something about how the last frontier was soon to be gone. We saw big tree-crunching machines drag chains across the forest, knocking down all the wood. We saw fires that were so big the smoke from them made rain clouds. We saw Indians dying from diseases they had no immunities for, and we didn't care; then we saw them fishing with dynamite.

The fish were sledgehammered off their feet.

We walk through the woods through the dark, Frank and I.

Knocked dumber than fence posts.

Frank holds on to my arm.

They breached like blown-up submarines.

I think he thinks I'm keeping him from falling.

■

It was a log jam on the pond.

At the barbed wire, we roll under the bottom strand.

I looked down, feeling in my heart triumphant as the U-boat blaster, who was my father, looking down at the oil slick, the life vests, and the spilled breakfasts of the men below.

The grass is dead and the frog piss frozen.

I said, "Deep-sixed is what you been."

With no paper, and me forgetting how to talk, we are the same as silent.

When I realized I hadn't heard what I had just said, I turned and saw Punky dripping all over and Frank stumbling with his hands out in front of him.

Ice is running on the water.

Our living trophy fish went rotten in the August sun. A dump truck hauled them away.

We slide down the dirt bank to the edge of the hatchery pond. I tell Frank what it looks like, but he shakes his head. I tell him there is no paper, but he shakes his head again. I show him where to write on my hand. What he writes on my hand is that he can no longer understand me. It leaves me Look Out high on a maybe-it-will-maybe-it-won't branch, feeling as if I could fall out of the biggest tree.

To save myself, I hit him on the face, knocking him backward through the sheeted pond. I wade to him and say,

"Hit me here, hit me here, hit me here." He can't understand me but he understands enough. I move closer, saying, "Harder, harder, harder." My legs break at the knees and I'm falling.

When the see-who-made-it-through-the-night light comes, we are still here. The pond is a quiet beyond no sound. I look up at the big empty and nowhere and it blurrs on me. What I'm thinking is that it didn't matter, that there is never anything we can do to save ourselves, that all of us always are dying of diseases that we have no immunities for.

Grave Digging

Sugarcane ash swirled out of the sky, collecting on the yellow umbrella, on the tape deck playing American music, on the surface of the water, on Augusto's cousin Kiko stretched out on an air mattress on the water, on Augusto's cousin Edison on the diving board, on Don Carlos, the gardener, trimming the grass with a machete, on Augusto.

Augusto knelt to the pool deck, doing forty-kilo wrist curls with a weight bar. He was muscled and tanned.

Seven-year-old Edison danced on his toes, his stick-doll arms looking as if they could break.

"Jump on me I'll cut your balls off," said Kiko.

Augusto looked at his cousins. They were so skinny. Skinny and weak.

"Jump," said Augusto.

"Goddamn Mondays," Kiko said.

Edison splashed into the pool.

"The club is closed. They haven't changed the movies. No chauffeur. There's nothing to do."

Water beaded on the fuzz above Kiko's lip.

Don Carlos worked barefoot, his pants cuffed above his ankles. The sun reflected off his cane-knife as he flicked it back and forth.

"Goddamn being stuck in the country," said Kiko. "In town we could at least play fútbol."

"It wouldn't matter, the curfew's still on," said Augusto. "You can't be more than three people in one place."

"I wish Mami and Papi were home," said Edison.

"When do they take the curfew off?" asked Kiko.

"When the guerrillas go," said Augusto.

"I'm not afraid of any guerrillas."

Don Carlos stood.

"I found the parrot," said Don Carlos.

Kiko and Edison scrambled from the pool. Blue and red and yellow feathers were scattered on the grass, as if someone had kicked over a painter's palette.

"What happened?" asked Kiko.

"Something just ate his head again," said Don Carlos.

"That's Octavio?" said Edison, standing in the grass with one pale foot on top of the other one.

"Guerrillas," said Kiko.

"Don't be stupid," said Augusto. "No guerrilla is going to cut off Octavio's head."

"They cut off your head so no one knows who you are," said Kiko.

Edison began to cry. Augusto couldn't believe Edison would cry like that, like a baby. And in front of the gardener.

"It's only a parrot," said Augusto.

"Abuelo is going to be mad when he gets home and there's no parrots left," said Kiko.

Augusto lay in what was once a Grace Lines deck chair, a present from some ship captain to Augusto's grandfather.

46

He shaded his eyes. The backyard of the hacienda was enclosed by a high stone wall lined with splintered glass embedded in cement. Orchid baskets and an empty parrot cage hung from the old Saman.

"But you had it all morning," said Edison, and he tried to push Kiko from the air mattress.

Kiko dunked Edison.

"That's not fair, you're not being fair."

A vulture, riding the ridge currents above the hacienda, soared, lost altitude, then pushed again with its wings.

"What about digging Indian graves?" said Augusto.

Augusto pointed to the ridge.

"I saw a hole that looks like it could be one."

"We never find anything," said Kiko.

"Where do you think all those artifacts came from?"

"Papi said we aren't allowed to go on the hill," said Edison. "Your dad said too."

"Yeah, they said that," said Kiko.

"I went running up there four times already."

"It's too dangerous," said Edison.

"Dangerous from what?"

Kiko shrugged.

"Guerrillas?" said Edison.

His own cousins. Babies and cowards. Even Kiko.

"You're just afraid," said Augusto.

"I'm not afraid," said Kiko.

"I'm not afraid," said Edison.

The maid brought out a tray with a pitcher of orange juice and three glasses. She was mestizo, thick across the nose and with a wide face.

"Melba, we're going to dig dead Indians," said Edison. "We're going to find gold and get rich."

"We need an expeditionary picnic lunch," said Augusto.

■

47

They drank orange juice and made a list of supplies.

"And we should take Suzi and Dogo for protection," said Edison.

Augusto went inside to use the kitchen phone. Melba was cutting bread for sandwiches. When Augusto picked up the receiver there was a dial tone.

"A miracle," said Augusto.

Augusto's girlfriend Cecilia wanted to go on the expedition also. And so did her friend, Luz Estela.

"Miss Fat and Complicated?" said Augusto.

The boys waited on the front porch with their grandfather's dogs. A tractor dragging a caravan of cane carts churned past on its way to the sugar mill.

Edison watched the road with a pair of military binoculars.

"I think the enemy is approaching," said Edison.

A white Mercedes turned through the gate and pulled up the stone drive. Cecilia jumped from the back seat.

"Hello, people," said Cecilia. "Are you ready?"

"We've been waiting," said Edison.

Cecilia had blonde hair and long legs and was wearing an American baseball cap. She kissed Augusto. The chauffeur opened Luz Estela's door.

"They're stopping everyone on the highway," said Luz Estela. "Somebody got disappeared and they're searching all the cars."

Luz Estela was fat. Fat lips, fat cheeks, fat everything. She kissed Augusto.

"Hello, Augusto love," said Luz Estela.

"Hello," said Augusto.

"Are we ready for our expedition?" asked Luz Estela.

"It's a long way up and hot," said Augusto.

"I bet I'm the first one to the top," said Luz Estela. "I brought my Uniroyal Croydons."

She lifted one foot to show off a new white tennis shoe.

■

Melba had packed their lunch into a huge picnic basket.

"What's in here, stones?" asked Augusto.

"I put three Cokes for everyone," said Melba.

"This is a problem," said Augusto.

"We could divide it up," said Cecilia.

"Don Carlos could bring it," said Kiko.

"Yeah, " said Edison. "Don Carlos."

Don Carlos lifted the padlock from the iron-spiked back gate. Augusto, shovel and rope across his shoulder, led the way, followed by Kiko carrying the other shovel and the tape player, Edison with a blue plastic bucket and his binoculars, the two dogs, Cecilia with a flashlight, and Luz Estela with her purse.

They crossed a dirt corral, an empty stream bed, and before they reached the bamboo they were strung out on the trail like an army patrol in the jungle.

"These stickers are ruining my new shoes," said Luz Estela.

Augusto walked faster. Edison hurried to catch up.

"Augusto, what happens when you get disappeared?"

Augusto kept walking. He slapped at a cloud of gnats. The cicadas screeched.

"You're just gone."

"But what happens? Where do you go?"

A boy Augusto had known at school, Ernesto Sanchez, he went to college and got disappeared.

"I think it's better not to know," said Augusto.

Augusto and Edison reached the hill bottom. They sat beneath a orange blossoming Tulipan. Suzi and Dogo slouched into the shade. They were from Argentina, bred to hunt wild boar on the pampas, and here in the tropics their albino skin was raw and ulcerated.

"Those dogs are sure goddamn ugly," said Augusto.

"Goddamn ugly," said Edison.

Luz Estela was last to reach the Tulipan. Her cheeks were splotchy red.

"How much farther?" she gasped.

The hill was badly over-grazed. Red soil spilled from cracks left by last winter's rains. More trees were missing. What did they do with the trees?

A herd of Zebu cattle moved across the slope. White egrets on the cows' backs swayed back and forth like miniature camel drivers. The dogs charged and the egrets took to the air.

"Suzi! Dogo!" yelled Augusto, and he picked up a stone.

"Maybe we should wait for Luz Estela," said Cecilia.

Augusto looked down the hill to where Luz Estela straggled.

"We'll be lucky if we don't have to carry her back," said Augusto.

"I'm not carrying her," said Kiko.

At the top of the ridge a lone Chiminango cast a dark spot on the parched grass. Near the tree was an eroded depression in the earth.

"That's it," said Augusto, dropping his shovel. "I don't know why I didn't see it before."

Kiko kicked at the sunken spot.

"It looks like somebody already dug it," said Kiko.

"Who's going to dig it? We're the only ones who know."

The dogs started over the backside of the ridge, toward the mountain.

"Suzi, Dogo, get over here," said Augusto.

He cut two lengths from the hemp rope and tied the dogs to the tree.

Augusto and Kiko began to dig. Cecilia sat in the shade.

"I'm ready with the bucket," said Edison.

Luz Estela struggled up the last little slope, her new shoes in her hands.

"I can't walk," said Luz Estela. "These Uniroyal Croydons have assassinated my feet."

She crawled beneath the tree.

"I think I'm dying."

Their legs were covered with streaks of the weathered red dirt. The hole was square, nearly a meter on each side. It became too deep for more than one of them to dig at a time. Kiko uncovered the first foothold.

"It's a grave for sure," said Augusto.

"I think it really is," said Kiko.

Edison abandoned the project to look at the valley through his binoculars. There was a line of cars on the highway.

"They're still stopping people," said Edison.

Smoke from the fields obscured the downtown part of the city. Only the poor barrios were visible, suspended above the smoke. The bull ring looked like a gray cement cup and saucer. At the country club the polo field was empty. Don Carlos was halfway up the hill.

"Here comes Don Carlos," said Edison. "He has the basket in the wheelbarrow."

Kiko climbed out of the hole.

"What?" said Augusto. "You just started your shift."

"I'm hot," said Kiko.

Don Carlos was bent by the weight of the wheelbarrow, his face a dark space in the shadow of his straw hat. A machete scabbard with colored tassels hung from his belt.

"Don Carlos, Don Carlos," shouted Edison. "I saw you with my binoculars."

Don Carlos parked the wheelbarrow under the tree.

"We're so thirsty," said Edison.

Cecilia and Luz Estela unpacked the food.

"Maybe Don Carlos can help dig," said Edison. "He's good at digging."

Don Carlos took his hat off. His gray hair was damp and plastered against his head.

"It's an Indian grave," said Kiko. "If we get rich we'll give you some."

They ate sandwiches and fruit salad from plastic plates, and drank Coca-Colas. Edison poured a Coke into one of the plates and set it in front of the dogs.

"Someone cut the head off that Perez-Garcia in the plaza," said Luz Estela.

"What?"

"With a torch thing; like what they use to rob banks."

"The sons of bitches," said Augusto. "That guy's our ancestor."

"Your ancestor?"

"Our great-grandfather was a Perez-Garcia."

"Wow," said Luz Estela. "I didn't know that. Didn't he find this place?"

"Sure he did," said Kiko.

"Guess what?" said Edison. "We found Abuelo's parrot without a head."

"Another one?" said Cecilia. "Didn't that happen already?"

"They only took his head again."

"All this no head business gives me the creeps," said Cecilia.

Don Carlos was a better digger than the boys. By the time they thought their stomachs were finished digesting he had disappeared into the earth.

"Don Carlos, come up, we're ready to dig again," said Edison.

Don Carlos climbed from the hole.

"You dug a lot," said Edison.

"Thanks, Don Carlos," said Augusto. "Thanks for the digging."

Luz Estela was asleep on the tablecloth. Cecilia had put the picnic trash and the empty Coke bottles back into the basket. Don Carlos set the basket in the wheelbarrow, lifted the handles, and started down the hill.

"Goodbye, Don Carlos, goodbye," said Edison.

"Goodbye," said Don Carlos.

"Thank you for the Coca-Colas," said Edison. "You saved our lives for sure."

The hole was too deep for them to throw out the dirt with their shovels. They tied the rope to the bucket.

"It's like the hot country down here," said Augusto.

"I'm head engineer," said Edison. "Dig, dig, we only have three hours light."

"You want some excavating music?" asked Cecilia. "We have salsa, rock, or that French bongo stuff."

Kiko climbed into the hole to take Augusto's place.

"Augusto, who were the Indians?" asked Edison.

"The people who lived here before us."

"What happened to them?"

Augusto dumped out the bucket.

"They died."

"How did they die?"

"Some of them died fighting the conquistadors."

"Perez-Garcia kicked their asses," said Kiko.

Their shadows were long on the hillside dirt.

"I'm tired," said Edison.

Augusto finished filling the bucket.

"Take it up."

"I'm really tired," Edison said.

"Maybe we should finish tomorrow," said Cecilia.

"Tomorrow?" said Augusto. "Somebody might steal everything."

"Are we there yet?" asked Luz Estela.

Still barefoot, she picked her way over to the hole.

"Ouch, ouch," said Luz Estela.

She looked down at Augusto.

"Wow, so deep."

"Sleeping beauty awakes," said Augusto.

"This one was probably for a king," said Kiko. "They made those deeper."

"I hope there is gold," said Luz Estela.

She turned a full circle.

"Where's the gardener?"

"He left."

"He left?" said Luz Estela. "I was going to pay him to carry me down in that wheel thing. I can't believe it. Now how am I going to get back down?"

Luz Estela sat in the dirt.

"Augusto, you were a brute to bring us up here," said Luz Estela.

The tape deck batteries had gone dead. The grave shaft was four meters deep and Kiko was nearly lost in the dim light at the bottom.

"Man, this is like being a prisoner of war," said Kiko. "This is like what they make you do."

The others crouched around the mouth of the hole.

"Don't Cecilia and Luz Estela need to leave if they'll be home before night time curfew?" asked Kiko.

"Keep digging or come up," said Augusto.

"Okay, okay," said Kiko.

"It is getting dark," said Cecilia.

"If you want to go, go, I'll stay and do it myself," said Augusto.

Augusto tugged at the rope.

"Isn't it full yet?"

"I don't think there's any dead Indians down here," said Kiko. "My shovel won't go any deeper."

"It's hard?" asked Augusto. "If it's hard it means we're at the bottom. The entrance is on the side."

"What side?"

"Any side, it's one of them."

Kiko dug into the wall facing him but it was like stone. He tried the wall at his back and with hardly a touch the dirt fell away.

"I found it," shouted Kiko. "I found it."

He flicked on the flashlight.

"There's a tunnel."

"Go inside," said Augusto.

Suzi and Dogo were on their feet, pulling at their rope leashes, straining toward the hole.

"You think it's okay?" asked Kiko. "You think it won't cave in?"

"Sure it's okay," said Augusto. "It's been okay for about a thousand years."

Kiko climbed out of the grave shaft.

"What?"

"It smells bad," said Kiko.

"It's supposed to smell bad, it's a grave," said Augusto. "What did you think?"

The dogs were choking themselves against their leashes.

"Those dogs are crazy," said Cecilia.

Augusto felt for the footholds. Cowards, all my family are babies and cowards. The air at the bottom of the grave shaft did smell bad. He stopped breathing through his nose. He pushed the bucket out of the way, picked up the flashlight, and stuck his head into the tunnel.

"Bones," said Augusto, his voice muffled.

"Bones? What kind of bones?"

"They look like people bones," said Augusto.

The flashlight beam reflected off of something.

"Hey, there's something metal."

"Gold? Is it gold?" asked Luz Estela.

"I'm going in."

55

"Be careful," said Cecilia.

Augusto, flashlight between his teeth, pulled himself forward into the tunnel, pushing off the far side of the grave shaft wall. He felt as if he were crawling into the throat of something. If you got stuck in here, if it caved in, you would suffocate. He breathed through his nose by mistake and almost had to spit the flashlight from his mouth.

They watched his legs disappear.

"Be careful," said Cecilia.

The dirt ceiling of the burial chamber crowded down on him. He crawled forward on his knees, careful to not touch the skeleton beneath him.

"What is it? What did you find?"

The shiny thing. He picked it up. A pocket knife? That was funny. How did a pocketknife get down here? And Augusto had seen this pocketknife a hundred times before. He turned it over.

"Well?"

Augusto turned back toward the tunnel entrance.

"You won't believe whose knife I just found," said Augusto.

"What did you say?"

The flashlight illuminated the far end of the burial chamber.

"Ahh," said Augusto, and he dropped the knife.

In the far corner, in a heap, were more dead people. But these dead people weren't skeletons yet; their heads still had hair, and their hands still had skin, and they were wearing blue jeans and shoes, and one of them had on a Mickey Mouse T-shirt.

Augusto jerked upright and was knocked back to his knees by the low earth ceiling. The flashlight fell. Darkness. Loose dirt streamed down on him.

"Ah, ah, ah," said Augusto.

"What?"

Augusto jabbed at the walls, searching for the tunnel

entrance. He found it. His legs had nothing to push off of. He should have gone out feet first. He was kicking the skeleton to pieces. He was going to be stuck. He dug at the tunnel with his fingers, dragging himself forward until he hit his head against the bucket.

"Are you coming up?" asked Kiko.

"Did you find something?"

Augusto fell out into the darkness of the ridge.

"Hey," said Kiko. "Watch out."

The fires in the valley, the black silhouette of the mountain, the tree, the dogs, all of it was spinning.

Augusto shoved Kiko and Luz Estela and Cecilia from the edge of the hole. He pushed Edison by his head.

"Stop it, stop it," said Edison.

"What's the matter with him?" asked Luz Estela.

The dogs snapped at the air. They lunged for the grave shaft, jerking themselves off their feet, thudding to the ground.

"What, what?"

We didn't find anything. We didn't, we didn't.

Augusto, making grunting noises, shoveled dirt back into the hole. He lost his balance and nearly fell in himself. He dropped the shovel. He was on his knees, pushing the dirt with his hands.

"Augusto, are you crazy?" asked Cecilia.

Augusto stopped throwing dirt. He tried to stand but his legs wouldn't hold him. He covered his face with his hands.

"Talk," said Cecilia. "Talk, talk."

"There's people," Augusto said. "Dead people."

"But it's a grave," said Cecilia.

"Not Indians," said Augusto.

"What?" said Cecilia. "What?"

"People," said Augusto. "Blue jeans. A Mickey T-shirt. It's regular people."

■

Augusto stumbled. He could no longer make out the silhouettes of the others. Suzi and Dogo ran loose, swooping over the hill like dog ghosts, spooking up clumps of cattle. Tio Pepe said not to come up here, my dad said too. We left the shovels, we have to go back for the shovels. They'll want to know where the shovels are. And the bucket. We left everything. He tripped again, falling.

The clanging was gone from Augusto's ears, the night silent except for his own jerky breathing. He sat where he had fallen, knees to his chest, holding himself, rocking, rocking. The cane fields blazed in widening lakes, shooting up showers of sparks, running together on the dark. Flames reflected off the smoke so that even the air appeared to be burning, and it seemed to Augusto as if his whole valley were on fire. He blinked and blinked his eyes.

Horizontal Light

Pop . . . pop . . . pop. Early in the morning the toads hug the pavement, looking for yesterday's sun. When I hit them square they bust like balloons, and when I just graze them they exhale like old people sighing when someone has died too young. I zip past hissing anhydrous ammonia tanks, white as buffalo leg bones, and accelerate to get out of Texas before the asphalt is gummy from the heat.

It has been one hundred degrees in Muleshoe for a month. I have worked the whole summer for my uncle, irrigating feed corn and painting grain silos and fertilizer bins. When I paint I paint everything white, and try not to think about Leigh. But she is in that paint, pale as the triangles of skin that her swimming suit shades from the sun.

It takes me twenty-two minutes to cross the Oklahoma Panhandle, and then it is Kansas until after lunch. I'm leaving before harvest, heading back to see Kris and Leigh. The plains of Colorado look like Texas until the mountains jump out of nowhere. Twenty miles from Fort Collins I see the pile of whitewashed rocks that shape a big A on the foothill above the stadium. It used to stand for the Aggies of Colorado State University. They're not Aggies anymore, now they're Rams. Kris and I have been talking about adding two S's to that A ever since we were kids. Only thing is it would be a lot of work.

At the farm Kris has planted barley right up to the road and it's ready for a combine. The lawn has just been cut and the mower squats in the clippings. Kris and Leigh are on the back porch.

"Hey," I shout.

"Yahoo," says Kris.

Skinny as a Mexican chicken, Kris has knotty farmer's muscles. He's got on ragged overalls and there are streaks of sweat running from his armpits. I hug him and walk to Leigh. She looks like she is watching a movie that she just decided to walk out of. She squeezes my hand and I kiss her, giving her a faraway hug. She has that same talc-like smell, and there is no hair on her arms which are covered with fine white scars.

"Hi," says Leigh.

"Missed you," I say to them.

"We missed you too," says Kris.

I look at the mountain which is turning blue as the sun tries to get behind it.

"You just get in?" asks Kris.

"Straight off the highway."

"From Texas?"

"Tex ass."

Kris's mother hugs me and tells me how much she missed me. How she thought about me when the TV said how hot it was in Texas, and how she wished I had stayed in Fort Collins. She fixes iced tea and we sit at the table next to the bay window.

"Where's your dad?" I ask Kris.

"Getting trucks to bring the cattle down from Soapstone."

I don't mind the old man not being around, he's not too fond of me.

"Isn't it kind of early?"

"We're ready to cut barley," says Kris. "We'll let them graze the stubble."

Kris asks me if I want to help fix a fence before it gets dark. I bring in my bag which has my work clothes in it and Kris's mother tells me to put it in the upstairs guest room. She says the bed is made and I am welcome to stay as long as I want. I tell her I will only stay a night or two, until I find a place in town. I put on my boots and go back downstairs. Kris and Leigh are together on the porch; they burst apart like startled pheasants.

"Let's go," I say.

We walk to the barn, booting up swirls of dust with our feet. Kris says it hasn't rained in three weeks. We throw a come-along, wire, and fence posts into the back of the Impala that Kris uses as a pickup. It's strange driving to the field with Leigh between us and her leaning toward Kris, but reaching to touch my knee so that my whole leg is nervous. We hit the bar ditch and head across the bottom where we always get stuck when it rains. The fence follows the lay of the land, separating the alfalfa and barley. I have fixed this fence about a hundred times. The alfalfa is long and nearly ready for the last cutting. Kris stops where the barbed wire is torn away from the posts. It's curled on the ground like a scorpion spiking itself in the back. The small cloud of earth following us swallows the car and then drifts across the field. The sun is low and bounces off the mountain and the little snow that always makes it through August. We open the doors but stay in the car. It's the choice part of a summer day, after it has started to cool off and some wind comes down from Wyoming.

"Better do it," says Kris.

We put our gloves on, cut away the bad wire, and pull up

the crooked fence posts. Leigh walks into the field to sight the fence line for us and she waves to me when I've got it right. When I wave back she is already looking off toward Greeley.

"How was Texas?" asks Kris.

"Hot," I say, "Corn grew so hard the fumes made me high."

"Hot," says Kris.

"How about here?" I ask him.

"Just about a regular summer," he says.

"How's things with Leigh?"

"It's been good."

"She looks awful good."

I wallop a new fence post with the sledge while Kris holds it at the base. The deep clay thumps, and soon I'm sweating. I arch my back and give all my body to the hammer. I want to show Kris and Leigh my summer muscle. The thud of each swing shakes me to my shoulders. When the post is in, Kris grabs my biceps and squeezes hard.

We get the five strands strung tight as banjo strings. I pluck them with a pair of pliers and listen to the twang bounce between the fence posts. We have set the fence straight and it looks right. Leigh is on the hood of the Impala, and Kris and I stretch out next to her. On the inside of her right knee she's still got this beauty of a scar from when we dumped my dirt bike riding up the canyon. She got her leg stuck under the muffler and I couldn't get the bike off her before I smelled the skin burning.

"You still got that scar," I say, pointing at it.

"I got this feeling it's not going away," she says.

The sun is giving that long horizontal light, a light that makes it seem like the colors are coming from the inside. We are silent, like we are seeing it all for the first time.

When that light is gone I strain to keep the feeling. A song I remember from somewhere comes on the radio. Leigh stands on the hood to dance, bouncing the shocks. We watch her, smiling and letting our heads roll back and forth on the windshield. I get up to dance with Leigh, and we rock the car and bump our hips.

"You hear something?" I ask Leigh.

Kris turns down the radio and I hear the shouting better but I can't locate where it is coming from.

"GODDAMN."

It's coming from the beans. I see Kris's dad, his arms flapping in the air like a crazy man and his feet coming off the ground. He looks like a silent movie, only I can hear him.

"GET OFF THAT CAR."

"Who said that?" asks Kris.

"I think it's your dad, he's in the beans."

"CRAZY DRUNKS," shouts Kris's father.

I jump from the car and help Leigh down. Kris takes a long look at the bean field.

"That's dad," says Kris.

"You think we're in trouble?" asks Leigh.

We watch the old man walk back to the house. Kris says not to worry, the folks are going out for dinner and will be gone soon. We stay in the field until they leave. It's late summer so even when the sun is gone the warmth stays. I put my arms behind my head and close my eyes and breathe in the smell of Leigh.

We drive up to the house and park by the water well. It is quiet except for the hiss of big trucks on the highway. The floodlight on top of the barn is on. It's above the basketball goal, and the shadow of the rim spreads like a water stain on the dirt.

"Game?" asks Kris.

We look in the tool shed for the ball. It's kind of flat. We try to locate a needle, but we don't find one. Leigh sits under one of the dying oak trees to watch us. When Kris takes it to the basket the first time, I know we're not holding back.

"One nothing," says Kris.

We play until we are sweating hard and tied at tens. Then Kris drives on me and smacks me in the mouth with his elbow as he goes by. I hear my teeth chatter and I come down holding my jaw. He knows he has hurt me and he stands next to me as I lean over, spitting blood on the ground.

"You right?" he asks.

I straighten up and wipe my mouth on my shirt. Leigh is walking toward the house. The grass is still tall enough to make her look barefoot.

"I'm going to see what there is for dinner," she says.

Kris holds the ball against his hip and watches her.

"She's mad," says Kris.

"Your ball," I say.

I'm no good with my hurting mouth. Kris has me down point-thirteen when he pulls up for a jumper. He's a skinny bastard but he has the best-looking jump shot of any white person who's ever left the ground. He goes up and I go with him. He's holding the ball way above his head and his wrist is cocked, loose and easy. He's still going up when I peak, and he keeps going like he is going to jump right through the sky. I owe him a good foul. Down I come and there is Kris, silhouetted against the mountain, sweat glistening off his body, and I realize I am probably seeing the most beautiful thing I will ever see in my whole life. He lets go of the ball and I don't even turn because I know it will click the net.

"Game," says Kris.

"Game," I reply.

We sit on the slab of the empty corn crib, and lean back against the wire.

"Guess you're slowing down, old man," says Kris.

"I was just letting you look good in front of your woman," I tell him.

We find Leigh sitting in the kitchen, in the dark, staring out the bay window at nothing but dark.

"You want to know who won?" asks Kris.

"No," she replies.

"He won," I say.

Kris turns on the light and we sit at the table with Leigh. I think she has been crying. I can't tell if Kris notices.

"What do you want for dinner? There's meat," says Leigh.

"Why don't we do a barbecue?" I say.

"I'd like that," says Leigh.

Kris and I go looking for charcoal. Kris says they had barbecues all summer long. I tell him that in Texas we never did find the grill, it was just that kind of summer. We go through the barn and the garage and don't find a bit of charcoal. Finally we end up getting out the axe to shave splinters from some winter wood.

"This'll be a real barbecue," says Kris.

Messing around the wood pile I find cedar scraps. There isn't anything I would rather smell burning than cedar. I bust the wood with the axe. Somehow I jolt myself and my mouth starts bleeding again.

"What?" asks Kris.

"Mouth's bleeding again."

I leave Kris to finish the wood and I go to fix my mouth. When I get to the house I don't even stick my head in the kitchen but go straight to the downstairs bathroom. I'm nearly through cleaning my mouth when I see Leigh standing in the hallway watching my reflection in the mirror. I don't say anything but finish and then go out in the hallway and look at her.

"How are you?" I ask her.

"Same as always."

She always says that, she would say that even if she had just won a million bucks.

"How's your mouth?" she asks.

"It's nothing."

"I don't think he meant to do it," she says.

"He didn't mean to do it."

We go to the kitchen and I sit down and watch Leigh cut the meat. We can see Kris dumping an armful of wood into the grill.

"That new muscle looks good on you," says Leigh.

By the time we have a decent cooking fire going Leigh has had the steaks ready a long time. We put the meat on and soon it's dripping and making flames burst up from the coals. Kris hangs a speaker out the kitchen window and we sit back in lawn chairs, listening to music from when we were in high school. We have a couple beers and by the time the meat is cooked I'm feeling better.

Leigh finds some leftover potato salad in the refrigerator and we end up having a real meal. When I finish eating, I prop my feet up on the grill. The heat feels good through my boots. Leigh says she wants to take a shower. I think she is trying to give Kris and me some time alone, either that or I am just making her nervous.

Kris and I walk to the corral, kicking at the stones on the dusty earth. We lean against the long wood and watch a jack rabbit sniff the air. When Kris sighs the old jack takes about a ten-foot leap and is gone.

"Olympic jack rabbit," says Kris.

The moon is up and hanging out east like a peach.

"You want some watermelon?" asks Kris.

We stumble around the tomato stakes and squash in the garden. I hunker down to the ground, pulling at the clods of earth with my hands. I can feel this dirt in me, under my fingernails, in my breath.

"I guess I better be leaving tonight," I say.

"You don't have to."

"Your dad's never too happy with me hanging around," I say. "After that car bouncing he'll probably be looking for it."

"I got a monster," says Kris, and I hear him pop the vine. It's a clean snap, the kind that tells you the melon is ready.

66

∎

When Leigh finds us our faces and bellies are covered in watermelon juice, and we are surrounded by seeds that look like June bugs crawling on the cement. Leigh looks great. She's the only girl I know who would look good stepping out of a car wreck. She has her hair wrapped up in a white towel, like some kind of wild Arab woman. I tell her I'm not staying.

"Where are you going to stay?" she asks me.

"I'll find a place, somebody'll be home."

Leigh sits between us, not close to either one of us. We sit for a long time.

Dexter Plays
Five Hundred

SIX KID SHADOWS and one man-in-a-wheelchair shadow stretch huge across the outfield grass. Dexter, glove between his teeth, wheels madly one way and then the other. Farmer Will stands at home plate, bat on his shoulder, the backstop printed across his back and all the way to the pitcher's mound. He chops a short ground ball and six kids chased by giants skid in on it. One of the Sams, the little one, snags it.

"Bounced four times," says Crying Poco.

"No points," says the other Sam.

Dexter spits out his glove.

"Ho, ho, ho," yells Dexter. "He can't hit."

The little Sam throws the ball back into Farmer Will, who hangs it out in front of himself, and this time kongs it.

"Four," yells Dexter.

The baseball passes over the six upbent faces tilted back like the faces of lost children in a crowd. It slices left and

Dexter, glove now on his hand, wheels after it. The ball drops fast and it seems impossible that Dexter will catch it. He leans and then stretches and at the last moment, in a lunge, he throws himself from the wheelchair and disappears in a cartwheeling of Dexter and wheelchair, baseball and glove, dust and shadow.

There is a long moment as the dust settles, Farmer Will dropping the bat and starting toward Dexter, and then, in the falling light, Dexter raises his mitt with the baseball in the webbing.

"Ho, ho, ho," says Dexter. "One hundred for the good guys."

Dexter, propped on an elbow, turns and looks for Katie on her hill. She's not there. He feels an emptiness he didn't know he could feel. What is it? Is this a hurt heart because she's not there? She's a kid, Dexter, says Dexter to himself. Then he sees that she is halfway down the slope, caught between her hilltop and where he has fallen. Dexter feels outside of himself. He feels as if he is on the hill, with Katie, looking down on this old guy in a wheelchair. An old guy in a wheelchair, says Dexter to himself. He looks away. "This kid's a mess," is what she whispered in his ear. Me too, thinks Dexter, I'm a mess too.

Six kids and six kid shadows converge on Dexter but pull up short before they touch his crashed chair. They have never touched his chair.

"Well get me back inside the thing," says Dexter.

The twisted mesquites and the horse barn and the white soccer goals and the barbed-wire fences and the tile bridge and Snugglebunny and the horses and Farmer Will's garden and the new kid Pilot on the runway and the white chalk lines on the baseball diamond reflect less and less of the less and less light, pulling themselves inside of themselves, drawing up their night blankets.

On the outfield grass the Five Hundred players are becoming their own shadows. The sound of the bat on the ball narrows on the near darkness, and the players, their movements hesitant, strain to see the direction of the ball's flight. They make last-second dives to catch it.

"You see it?"

"I caught it, I caught it, three seventy-five."

"On the bounce? On the bounce?"

"One bounce."

The pitch of their voices changes. It has become a game of defending yourself. Now they are targets. None of them wants to be the first to quit.

"Get your teeth knocked out."

"Call this game suicide."

They began to disappear even from each other. A crack of the bat and nobody moves.

"Where'd it go?"

"Anybody see it?"

No answer. They wait and listen. Nothing.

"Okay," yells Dexter. "That's it. Don't shoot, Farmer, we're coming in."

They gather at the backstop and drop mitts and bats into the duffel bag, and then start across the playing field dark. At the hillside bottom Dexter turns to take the switchback road cut into the slope. The others climb straight up into the dark. Farmer Will hesitates.

"Go ahead," says Dexter. "I got it."

The road is really just a track wide enough for Bucky to get the Ford 5000 and the drag-mower down to cut the playing field grass. From the flat next to the bridge it rises north to south for a hundred yards, then the switchback and another hundred yards to the hilltop. Dexter leans his shoulders into his wheels. The bladed earth, channeled and eroded by rains past, jars Dexter's wheels.

"One, two," says Dexter as he pushes.

What are you? thinks Dexter. Thirty-eight? Thirty-eight, right? I'm thirty-eight. Forty-nine to fifty-nine, fifty-nine to sixty-nine, sixty-nine to seventy-nine. Thirty. And nine more. I'm thirty-nine?

When he realizes that he has been in the chair more years than he ever walked on his legs, it stops him dead in his wheelchair tracks. It sucks all the air from his lungs. He starts rolling backward before he realizes what is happening and grabs at the rims. Jesus, Jesus, more years than you ever walked on your own legs?

Dexter sets his brake, leans back, and looks up at the first stars, but he doesn't see anything. He can't seem to put any thought together. Jesus. His arms feel empty of muscle. More years than he ever walked on his legs? Where is he now? Halfway up a goddamn red dirt hill in West Texas. Still got the other half to go. This is not a bad dream you wake up from.

Dexter doesn't know how long he has been listening to his breathing. He takes deeper breaths, slows it down. Forget about all of that, thinks Dexter. Just forget about it and get up this hill. He takes the brake off. What else do you do? There's nothing else to do. Just push this old chair up the hill. More years than I ever walked on my legs. Jesus.

"One, two," says Dexter.

Dexter reaches the switchback, brakes his left wheel and spins the right one. He hits a rock and it nearly sends him over the edge. He jerks at the rims to save himself. Near death experience, thinks Dexter. That's what else there is to do. And you didn't want to go over that hill, you son of a bitch, see there, just now, you didn't want to die.

"One two, one two."

When Dexter makes the hilltop he stops in the dark, still outside of the reach of the last of the pink street lamps. He wipes the sweat from his eyes. The thudding of his heart seems to fill the whole night.

"You sounded like a train coming up that hill," says a Katie voice out of the dark.

Dexter wheels himself toward where the Katie voice came from.

"I think I can, I think I can," says Dexter.

He sees her outline leaning back against the fallen lamp pole. He stops at Katie's feet.

"Grab my legs?" asks Dexter.

Katie lifts Dexter's legs at the calves.

"Here we go," says Dexter.

Dexter lifts himself over the side of the wheelchair, bracing one hand on the armrest, the other on the fallen lamp pole, and then he lowers his body to the grass.

"Got it from here," says Dexter.

With his palms facing downward, he moves his back up against the round cement. Katie sits next to him, close. He has a sense that they are on an island surrounded by dark.

"Five hundred," says Dexter, still breathing hard from the climb. "I was better at that game when I had legs."

It's an island of something different than dark. Dexter has the sense of a finite space.

"Saw you catch that ball," says Katie.

"You saw?"

"Thought maybe you killed yourself."

"No luck," says Dexter.

Dexter tilts his head back, leans on his elbows, looks up at the night, the stars brighter now, the banding of the Milky Way. More years in that chair than he ever spent on his own legs.

"The universe is expanding," says Dexter. "Everything zooming away from everything else."

Katie doesn't say anything to that.

"They can tell because the light from the other galaxies is red shifted. All moving away."

Dexter tilts his head back further, looking almost directly overhead.

"Except for that guy right there," says Dexter, pointing. "Right there, at Andromeda's knee, that misty spot, that's the Andromeda Nebula, and it's blue shifted, it's coming toward us."

"What happens?" asks Katie.

"What happens?"

"When it gets here."

"Don't worry," says Dexter. "It doesn't get here for about twenty billion years. We got other things to worry about."

Katie pulls her knees to her chest, wrapping her arms around her knees, holding herself close.

"Why did you stop on the hill?" asks Katie.

Dexter looks up again, sees the Goat, the Water Carrier, only Fomalhaut showing in the Southern Fish, though they are deep into Autumn now.

"I was remembering a girl," says Dexter. "There was a girl who lived two farms over. I used to watch the stars with her."

He doesn't know why he has just said this, why he didn't tell her about the more years in the wheelchair than on his own two legs. About that thought knocking all the air from his lungs. But it's true; there was a girl.

"Was she your girlfriend?" asks Katie.

"I guess so," says Dexter.

"When I'd go visit her I had to walk across two big cotton fields in the dark," says Dexter. "We'd lay on top of the old water tank where nobody could see us. It would still be warm from the sun."

"What happened to her?" asks Katie.

"I think she still lives there. Where I grew up."

"Do you ever talk to her?"

"Not for a long time," says Dexter.

"Are you sad?" asks Katie.

"That you didn't marry her?" says Katie. "That she's not your wife?"

Dexter doesn't know what to answer. He looks up at his

stars, breaths in the smell of the red dirt, the smell of the grass, the smell of Katie again. Am I sad? thinks Dexter. He feels lost more than he feels sad. They sit for a long time. He watches Hercules walk right off the night.

"Sometimes I'm sad," says Dexter. "About some things. But right now I'm not sad."

"If I could wish for anything," says Katie. "If I saw a star fall right now, I'd wish that you would never be sad."

There is a warmth in the air that holds itself. Dexter has a sense of a moment caught, a moment held. He strains to not lose it, as if he is stretching every muscle in his body to catch that baseball, straining, straining, reaching to hold it before it drops away.

Playing Iwo Jima

What I am doing now is I am butt-welded to a John Deere 4020, unzipping the earth west of Muleshoe, lifting her dusty dress. I am probably alone out here, only who knows? I will put it together for you the way I put it together for myself. There is heat waving off my tractor's fenders, dust devils jumping the farm to market, and Sarah waiting in the turn row with a bag full of Ogallala water. Sarah waiting in the turn row is the only part of this that is for sure a lie. There is no question I am plowing the beaches of Iwo Jima, turning up bones from Frog Wars already fifteen years ago.

The rules were that there weren't any rules, but if you got frog on you you were dead. I had no arm, Harold called me woman, so mostly I was dead. When they picked armies, Jap and Marine, I was last—last to go, even after Sarah. The Japs defended the milk barn, Iwo Jima, and the Marines waded ashore through the cotton. You combated with a pocket full of Black Cats, a pocket full of frogs, and a punk between your teeth. The punk's glow gave you away, but when you torched that fuse it was like pulling a pin. Stick a finger-thick Black Cat in old frog's mouth, make him look cigar-smoking, torch the fuse, and hurl that frog grenade across the West Texas sky. Last-ditch assaults were pure carnage, frog bombs dropping everywhere. When you got a direct hit, you would say, "Take that, fuckhead, I frogged your ass!" And if they got you, you would say, "Oh fuck, I been frogged!"

When I did my firefly-smeared-on-cement imitation, when I sparklered across the Delta's high black tent, I said, "Oh fuck, I been frogged." I was in my baby Piper with thirty-foot mufflers and exhaust shields. I was hawking, not making a noise, except my prop soft-chewing the Mekong muck. I was looking for somebody's ass to frog when they frogged my own. It was all swirling smoke. I grabbed my sky blanket and went looking for a door. I thought, This is what they call difficulty leaving the aircraft, and I tried to remember what they said about that. I couldn't see to see until the phosphorus lit. Then I saw myself reflected on the air like it was a mirror, a mirror of me and a mirror of Harold the night of the Frog War to End All Frog Wars.

Flashbulb-caught is how Harold looked the night of the Frog War to End All Frog Wars, which was also the night he frogged his own ass. It was the day after the Fourth of July. We had gunpowder enough to blow away half the farm, and the wind was blowing warm through the tree strip. The run had been made to the tail-water pit, what we called the ammo dump, where the frogs were, and we had grenades for days. Sarah was chosen a Jap and me a Marine, so I resigned myself to battle. It was dark already and the moon was shining off the tin tractor shed and the round water of the horse tank. Iwo Jima was just a black lump. We could hear

Japs talking bold, trying to make themselves brave because they did not know where we were coming from. Harold drew the plan in the dirt. The Marines with shoes would attack out of the orchard, what we called the mine field, where the goatheads were. Harold and I, the only barefoots, we would commando out of the cotton when the mine-field attack had their attention.

I was flying over what I called the mine field in the Delta when they got my attention. I had that Delta laid out in my head just like our farm. There was the cotton patch, which was mostly friendly; the tractor shed and the horse tank, which about you never knew; and the mine field and Iwo Jima, which were always trouble. So when they direct-hit me, it wasn't that I wasn't expecting, but I wasn't expecting the phosphorus to do like it did. The phosphorus, what I called my party candles, was what I laid down on the so-called to-be-frogged asses. Where my candles landed, soon followed large amounts of destruction. What the phosphorus did was ash my retinas. It left me sideways to the world. What it does is, it doesn't let me see what is out in front.

When you are tractor-driving, it is what is out in front that counts. You decide what gets it and what doesn't, and what you leave behind can't be undone. My dad raised his boys to plow Kansas-straight straight lines. When I came back, all I could do was draw snakes on his fields. He put a roll bar on the tractor so if I back-flipped it I wouldn't kill myself, and started with his mirrors. The first year I plowed under half his cotton, but he didn't quit on me, and he finally got it so I could practically see what I was doing. Anymore, I'm just dangerous to fence post and irrigation pipe.

Waiting in the cotton for the mine-field attack to happen, I didn't feel dangerous to anything. I was a deserter in my heart. All I wanted was Sarah in the tree strip. Dead Marines and Japs both were supposed to bleed together in the tree strip until the war was over. Whenever Sarah got it first, I would frog myself to be with her. It undid Harold. He called Sarah a Jima-whore, and me a Marine-woman disgrace. When the first range rounds whomped in, raising dust, Harold and I crawled forward through the furrows, butt low, hunkered down on our faces. We gave the mine-field attack time to convince those Japs. Then we came out of the cotton, skirting the Case tractor broken down so long it was growing roots. We were in a charge so strong that even I thought we wouldn't be stopped. We had nearly made the wide-open when we went sprawling, howling to the ground. In a stroke of genius, in a tactic we had never known, the Japs had goathead-mined it. They threw frog down on us.

It is afternoon now and the sun has an angle on me so that when I am heading west my horizon is mostly orange. At the end of the field is a bar ditch. It is where my dad was laying when his brother came yelling through the dead cotton to tell him there had been a Pearl Harbor. My dad was resting his sights on a rabbit. He says it was the last unhuman thing he ever pointed a gun at. He says that jack got saved by a war. In the turn row, I lift my cultivator, and I am swallowed in a red-dirt storm. Plowed earth and blown-up earth smell the same to me. It is a tornado-shelter smell, a wet-cement smell, the frog breath in a Texas loblolly. The dust settles in my elbows as I head back toward where the dark is coming from.

When I was the boy called woman by Harold, I would thread two miles of that red dust and dark through my toes to watch Sarah pull a dress over her head. The dark between our place and their place was country dark. I walked the tree strip, listening to wind walk on trees, running when bull bats spooked up from the dirt. Sarah waited until she knew I was there, standing on the wheel rim against the outside wall. She opened the curtain so that mosquito screen was all that was between us. Then she pulled her dress over her head, and did her desert-place dance.

The day I left I asked Sarah to drive the farm with me. I wanted to take one last look, just in case. It was late summer, the growing was over, the well motors were quiet. We could hardly see the farm for the waist-high cotton and head-and-a-half field corn. I asked Sarah if she wanted to skip frogs on the tail-water pit for old times. She didn't say but walked on the dam and down to the water. I told her she looked so mighty in her white dress that it was what I would remember to come back to. She hung the white dress on the barbed wire of the fence. We lay down in the dirt, and I let her pour dirt over my head. She said we had to throw a penny in the water and say this-is-fors. We couldn't find one. All we could find was a lockjaw-rusty nail. Sarah dropped it in the tail water and said, "This is for you getting back here, and for everything staying the way it is."

The way it was was that Harold and I were completely routed from the field. We found ourselves belly in the cotton, listening to our retreating hearts on the dirt. Harold said we had been Dresdened. Dresdened, Dunkirked, and Waterlooed. In the humiliation of impending defeat, he decided to win the war with firepower. I followed him to the tractor shed, where he reached into the dead air space between the walls. His hand came out with a gunpowder-monster. He said he had engineered it himself, said it was the secret weapon, the one that would turn the tide, the atom frog-bomb. I asked if a bomb like that wouldn't be against the rules. Harold looked at me and said, "War is fair and all love."

■

When I came home from the real war, and Harold took me home to meet his wife, he had to lead me by the hand with the one hand he still has. When he turned in the drive and stopped short, I asked, "What?" He said she was standing there. I asked how she looked, and he said, "Same as always." I asked what she was wearing, and he said, "A white dress." I waited for something to happen. I asked Harold what was happening. He said, "Let's get out." I listened to him get out. Then I tried to remember what the rules were for difficulty leaving the aircraft, or anything. I waited until I wondered if I was alone. Then I felt her hand on my arm, and I said to myself, "You been frogged like you'll never know."

Harold said we were going to Hiroshima their asses. He said we had to search for a frog with a big enough mouth. We stalked the sides of the tail-water pit, slipping in mud as we groped with our hands. We took the biggest frog we found and pried open his mouth. He looked like he had been telephone-poled. Then Harold made his charge, rose up out of the cotton like the hordes himself, his black outline hanging on the end of a spark. When he pulled up to light the fuse, Harold looked bigger than life. He looked as bronze and as famous as that statue of the Marines lifting the flag. He was leaning back in a heave when the atom frog-bomb went off. He was flashbulb-caught, and then he disappeared in a shower of frog and finger mist.

The sun has gone where it goes to. The engine casing pops as it cools. I take off my boots and hang my pants on the barbed wire of the fence. Out in the middle of the tail-water pit, I can't get any hint of light, and I feel like I am swimming beneath the rim of a bomb crater. I dive down into it. With my fingers I sift through layers of bones on the bottom. What I am looking for, what I can't find here, is a tenpenny nail. When I come up for air, someone has killed the water well. It is the quiet of quiet after battle. All I can hear is breathing from the mud. I stand naked in the water. I try to wash myself with the soft caliche. I try to clean it from me. But what I have on me won't come off, what I think I have on me is frog for always.

The Weight
of the World

Big Tom touches the window sill. It's numbingly cold. Where I'm standing now is real, thinks Big Tom. His heart pounds, he tries to slow his breathing, tries to get the world back beneath his feet. That's what I get for playing mind catch with the medicine ball, thinks Big Tom. That's what Joey had called it. When what you were thinking knocked you off your feet the same way a medicine ball in the chest would. Jesus, Joey, says Big Tom in his head, I caught the medicine ball hard this morning.

"Tom?" says Rachel. "Tom, what?"

Thin winter light. It has snowed on Court Street and the rest of Brooklyn. The snow covers the sidewalk which is still empty of people. Steam swirls up from a wet manhole cover. In the distance a round green light marks an open subway station in the Heights.

"Tom, are you all right?" asks Rachel.

"A dream," says Big Tom. "I was dreaming."

He lies back down in the bed. Rachel puts her hand on his chest. He looks around the dim room as if it is all new to him. The dresser, his blue bathrobe hanging from a hook on the closet door, the lamp, Rachel's high-backed reading chair, Rachel's slippers warming beneath the radiator, and on the night table next to Rachel, pictures of their son and daughter-in-law and two grandchildren. We've been lucky, thinks Big Tom. If I were to die right now, it has been a good life. And there has to be a last time for everything.

Now Big Tom is in the bed alone. It's past time for getting up, but Big Tom doesn't feel like getting up. He feels tired is what he feels. What have I done to be tired for? thinks Big Tom. Nothing except for sleeping. Big Tom says to long dead Joey in his head, The last time Big Tom lifts the Weight of the World may have already happened.

"Tom, breakfast," says Rachel.

Big Tom has his elbows on the bright yellow tablecloth of the kitchen table. The kitchen smells of coffee. He looks out the window. It's snowing on Court Street again. A good life, thinks Big Tom, It's been a good life. So much good luck.

"Here's your toast," says Rachel.

She lifts the toast to his plate with a fork.

"Tom, what was it this morning?" asks Rachel.

"Just a dream," says Big Tom. "I was talking with Joey."

"Joey," says Rachel, and she covers one of Big Tom's hands with her own.

Big Tom looks at Rachel. Beautiful Rachel, no longer so beautiful, but still beautiful to Big Tom. She still has the girls, most all of the girls are still alive. Big Tom is the last of the boys.

His gym bag is in the front closet. It's the same bag he has always carried. In the bag are his gray sweats, a jump rope, and a weight belt.

83

"Maybe you shouldn't go, Tom," says Rachel. "The radio says it's going to snow all morning."

"Today is my benching day," says Big Tom.

"You could go tomorrow."

Big Tom folds a clean towel and puts it in the gym bag.

"People are going to think you're crazy," says Rachel. "They're going to find you wandering the streets and lock you up for your own good."

"I ought to lock you up because you're too good looking," says Big Tom.

"Tom," says Rachel, and she hugs him tight. "You be careful."

Big Tom, big no longer, takes the stoop steps less than one step at a time. Okay, legs, let's start walking, says Big Tom. He carries the gym bag over his shoulder. He walks with his face bent into his coat, the snow finding the skin beneath his eyes. There are all the morning's noises to hear. Paper trucks and bread trucks and early morning buses.

A boy shovels the sidewalk clean. He stops shoveling and rests his elbow on his shovel. Big Tom looks to where the boy is looking. A dark haired girl up high has opened a window, and she reaches her hand out to feel the snow. It's just any dark haired girl in a white T-shirt, but for Big Tom she is Rachel when Rachel was his girlfriend. He closes his eyes and sees Rachel leaning from the window of the five story walk-up, reaching to drop a purple sock folded over on itself and the key so that it will land softly. He sees this so clearly that he drops the gym bag and holds out his hands in front of him.

When Big Tom closes his hands on nothing and opens his eyes, he comes back from sixty years ago. He looks up to see the dark haired girl looking down at him. She holds herself with her arms as if she has just felt the cold for the first time.

Big Tom looks down and sees the gym bag at his feet. What am I doing here? Then he remembers. He picks up the gym bag. Jesus, Joey, says Big Tom, They're going to lock me up for my own good.

He passes the bakery with all the wedding cakes in the window. The snow is piled an inch high on the store's empty blue window boxes. When he turns the corner and the wind stands him almost straight up, he stops. What is this smell? What, what? Then he remembers. It's the smell of open ocean blowing in with the snow.

Big Tom remembers taking the train to see the ocean when he and Rachel were boyfriend and girlfriend. He liked it best in winter, when there weren't any people, and they could walk across the empty beach with the wind blowing across the sand and their faces. They would take their shoes off and walk down to where the sand was damp, and write I love yous in the sand with their toes. Sometimes they wrote right down to the water, so that what they wrote only lasted between one wave and the next. Let's kiss right here, Big Tom wrote. You want to kiss me? wrote Rachel, with a great big question mark. I want to take your clothes off, wrote Big Tom. All of them? wrote Rachel. And a wave caught her and splashed her dress.

Big Tom finds himself back on the street corner, the wind still blowing, the snow still falling. I lived here all my life, thinks Big Tom, For how long did I forget about the ocean?

He climbs the brick steps into the gym. The climb gives him the sound of a quick drumming speed bag in his ears. He stops twice to catch his breath. And this guy is going to lift the Weight of the World? Okay legs, let's go. He uses the hand railing to help himself inside. Sam is mopping the entry way. He is just about the last person that Big Tom knows here.

"Look what the storm blew in," says Sam.

Big Tom passes the scale he no longer uses, the scale he hasn't used for a long time. Big Tom and Joey had once been religious about weighing themselves. Then one day Joey said, This Toledo son of a bitch says we're disappearing. And neither one of them had ever stepped on a scale again.

The last time Big Tom saw Joey was the day Joey died. They benched just like any other day. In the afternoon they took the train to a Yankee game. They had beer and hot dogs and more beer. Rachel had been so mad when Big Tom got home late and couldn't get his key in the door. But that was the way to go. It was really just more good luck. A good life, a good lift, a Yankee game, the Yankees win, go to bed, and then you don't wake up. That was it for Joey.

Big Tom's locker has a strip of once white wrist-wrapping tape on it that reads: BIG TOM. The other lockers have names on them too, but these names no longer have faces for Big Tom. There is a puddle of water next to the wooden bench. Someone has already showered. Big Tom hangs his shirt and trowsers. He reaches for his sweats and is startled by the face of an old man in the combing mirror. Jesus, Joey, says Big Tom, That old guy staring back is me.

He is pulled to the weight room by the skip-skip whip-whip of jump ropes. Weights clang to the floor as someone unbalances a bar. Laughing. Rep counts. The sneezy smell of chalk.

A man picks up the fives and tens he spilled from the preacher curl. He looks up and sees Big Tom.

"Hello," he says.

"Hello," says Big Tom.

A thick-necked boy is benching, lifting four plates easy. The kid that reminds Big Tom of Joey is spotting him. This kid lifts and lifts and lifts and always looks the same.

"Hey," says the kid. "Want to jump in?"

"No, no," says Big Tom. "No, go ahead."

He moves away from them. He'll wait until they finish with the bench, until he can have the bench all to himself. The new mirrors leave him with no place else to look but at his feet. He waits and remembers Joey once reading a magazine and saying, Says here when the human body reaches thirty it begins the long decline. Sure, Big Tom had said, How about a spot. Joey, eating his breakfast apple, said, No matter what, it's downhill from here on out. We've peaked, said Big Tom. Shot our wad, said Joey. And they laughed. It had seemed funny when Big Tom could lift a bar with six plates, throw it in the air as if it had wings of its own. Big Tom, now the last of them, shakes his head and thinks, What did we know then?

They have finished with the bench. Big Tom slides a plate on to each end of the bar and locks them down with collars. This is the Weight of the World. A seven foot olympic bar, two big plates, and two collars. One hundred forty-five pounds all. They had all called it the Weight of the World; all of them except for Joey, who when he was alive was the skinniest, and could never lift anything, and he had called it the Weight of the Wife. It had once been nothing for Big Tom. It had been warm up, piece of cake, wrist curl for days. Today even the collars are heavy.

"Need a spot?"

The kid has come back. Big Tom knows he needs a spotter, but he knows more that he doesn't want anyone to see if he doesn't lift it.

"No, no thank you," says Big Tom.

"Thanks," Big Tom says.

Big Tom reaches his hands into the chalk bucket. Let's go Joey, today we're going to blast, says Big Tom. But he's not convinced. He lays himself down, the bench against his back. He feels as if he's inside a movie he has already seen. When he grips the bar, chalk motes silt down on him. This is it. He takes five quick breaths, then decides he's not ready. There's a last time for everything, says Big Tom to himself.

Okay, says Big Tom. He lifts the bar from the rack. It's heavy. He steadies it and lets the weight settle into his shoulders. He says to himself, When the lungs kick out the air, you throw the bar right through the roof. He lowers the bar into his chest, filling his lungs and readying for the push. One, two, three. Up. Up, up, up. Almost. But then the Weight of the World is pushing back harder. Uh-oh. The bar comes down rib-cracking hard. Help. Help, help, help. Nothing. Somebody better help, thinks Big Tom, Or I'm a goner.

When Big Tom looks up again he sees Joey lean to drop a purple sock that is rolled over on itself. Big Tom lets go of the bar to catch it. But when the bar nearly splits his chest in half, Big Tom understands that Joey isn't there to help him lift the Weight of the World. He says to himself, The son of a bitch is helping me into being dead is what he's doing.

Blood clangs in Big Tom's head, an endless stream of weights streaming off an unbalanced bar. All the air is gone from Big Tom's lungs and his eyes are not seeing anything. He feels a settling of his whole body the way he first settled the bar into his shoulders, and at first it is a good feeling, until he realizes that it's gravity settling him into his grave.

When the weight is gone from Big Tom's chest, he thinks that he may have died. Then he hears talking and he's glad to not be alone. It's dark, but then not as dark as before, and when his world stops spinning Big Tom sees that he is not in heaven or hell or any place else but the weight room of the gym. Faces peer down at him. He hears words that he can't make out.

The thick-necked kid still holds the bar which he has lifted from Big Tom's chest. The man from the preacher curl is there.

"Are you okay?" he asks Big Tom.

"Okay," says Big Tom.

It's all over, thinks Big Tom.

"Sure you're okay?"

There has to be a last time for everything. You just have to get up, thinks Big Tom. You just have to get up and get home.

"Sure," says Big Tom.

Big Tom gets himself upright on the bench. There is a

chalky taste in his mouth. He looks and sees the other lifters looking, shaking their heads, and he sees himself with Joey, all those years ago, watching an old man stumble away from the weight bench. The old man who had once been king of the weight room. They had watched for years as the weight slowly disappeared from his bar until all he was lifting was the bar alone. One day Joey had said, He's not going to get it. And he didn't. They lifted the bar from the old man's chest. He tried to stand, nearly fell over, then stumbled away. It was the saddest thing Big Tom had ever seen. He had said to Joey, The day I can't lift the Weight of the World is the last time this weight room sees me. Now Big Tom says to Joey, This is the saddest thing I've ever seen twice. Then he says, That's all she wrote for us, we're all gone.

Someone goes back to lifting, slapping plates on a bar. Big Tom is thankful. He leans, breathes, feels his feet against the floor. It's been a good life. But still, with all that luck, it's still come down to this. He takes deep breaths, gets ready to walk. Don't stumble on me now, says Big Tom to his legs. But they won't even stand him up.

Okay, says Big Tom, We'll wait a minute, then we'll go. He waits the minute. He waits one more. But even then his legs won't take him. Finally he understands what his legs are telling him. They are telling him that the lifting isn't over, that it's never over, that he has no place else to go.

When Big Tom can keep his feet underneath him, he stands, loosens the collars, and takes the big plates from the bar. Then he searches for the smaller ones, the thirty-fives. He slides them back on the bar and now the other lifters are watching. He knows they are watching, the room gone silent. He lays himself down on the bench. When he looks up he sees the skinny kid that reminds him of Joey.

"I'll spot you," says the kid.

Big Tom takes his breaths, dips the bar into his chest, but even this little weight seems to be pushing down harder than he can push back. He sees the kid's hands move under the bar and he shakes his head. Not yet, it's not over yet.

"You got it," says the kid.

Now the bar is moving up.

"It's all you," says the kid. "It's all you, it's all yours."

Big Tom feels the air kick out of his lungs and he pushes until he feels his arms lock out. He drops the bar on the rack.

"Take that you dirty death son of a bitch," says Big Tom.

Big Tom sits up slowly, blinking back the holes in what he's seeing.

"It was all you," says the kid.

Big Tom leans forward, with his elbows on his knees. Dizzied by the lift, he can only think that he needs a name for this new weight, this one small weight that has become so big, and then he thinks, this is the weight of my life now.

Retard Gigging

AUGUST, JIM FEELS IT ON HIM like trying to swim in clothes. A street cleaner plows by, stirs it up, hurts Jim's nose. It's an un-august August. There's a general lack of augustness in Jim's neighborhood. Augustly speaking, thinks Jim, someone should drop the biggest bomb.

Januaries, that's what he's dreaming of. And hoping they're not playing Creedmore. He can't believe he forgot to ask. Thirty bucks is thirty bucks, but if it's Creedmore, he's going back to bed. A Hoke honk from the curb. Jim unleans his guitar and himself. His Big Nikes stick off the pavement, like subway fat-ladies clicking their gum every chew.

"Nice haircut," says Hoke. "Get hit by a lawnmower?"

"Where we playing?" asks Jim. "Don't tell me Creedmore. If it's Creedmore I'm not coming."

"The good news is we aren't playing Creedmore," says Hoke.

Jim keeps his feet planted.

"Jump," says Hoke. "It's King's County, kid's stuff. Going to visit Mikey."

They shoot up Amsterdam to collect the Hanford. Running fifty between lights gets the muck to almost feeling like a breeze.

"Dripping out there," says Jim.

"Like Panama."

"What do you know about Panama?"

"I heard."

Hoke wears a torn up tear-away from when they were in high school. Still number twenty-two. Still has biceps like a weight lifter. And a pair of black eyes like he hasn't slept in a week.

"How's your dad?" asks Jim.

"Hanging," says Hoke. "Yesterday was kind of rough."

I'll go visit him this week, I will, thinks Jim.

"He keeps thinking he's back in the war," says Hoke.

"Yesterday," Hoke says. "He says to me, 'We're over the channel, I can see England, we're gonna make it back.' So I tell him, 'Yeah dad, we're gonna make it back.' "

"Deep," says Jim.

"Too deep for me," says Hoke. "I'm not ready for this shit."

My father will die too, thinks Jim.

The same stripped car as always is on Hanford's stoop, and the same junkie as always is asleep in the back seat.

"My accountant," Jim says, which is what he always says.

Hanford, called Mr. El Skin and Bones by Jim, tries to maneuver his Fender Rhodes between Hoke's drums and a snow shovel.

"Let's go Ethiopia, we're late," says Hoke.

"Middle of fucking August and he's still got a fucking snow shovel in here," says Hanford.

"Don't go any-fucking-where without my fucking snow shovel," says Hoke.

"Nice fucking neighborhood," says Jim. "Any fucking apartments for rent?"

"Funny," says Hanford.

Hanford gets in the back seat. He wipes his face with a handkerchief.

"You believe this weather?" says Hanford.

"It's humorous out there," says Jim.

"Tumorous," says Hoke.

West End Avenue and a leggy blonde stilettoes herself up the sidewalk.

"Oochi mama," says Hanford.

Hoke, staring hard, drives both sides of the street. This is how we die? thinks Jim.

"See that?" says Hoke, driving forward but looking backward. "The wheels of life."

Hoke punches at the empty space in the dash where the radio used to be.

"Rap master," says Hoke.

"Oh no," says Jim.

"Oochi mama, oochi mama, I got a pussy jones," raps Hoke. "Oochi mama, oochi mama, I can feel it in my bones."

"A hook," says Hoke. "Handyman, you hear it?"

"Dated," says Jim.

"Like a train wreck," says Hanford.

Jersey hangs across the Hudson like some kind of bad dream, the green H E S S letters on the oil storage tanks barely showing through. They dive under old elevated pieces of highway. Below 14th street wooden docks list into the river; sinking battleships sprawled with half-naked bodies trying to escape the heat. The tunnel is up to costing two-fifty so they take Chambers to the bridge.

The bridge is empty.

"Where's all the traffic?" asks Hoke.

"Don't look back," says Jim. "Maybe Manhattan got nuked."

"Stuck in Brooklyn the rest of your life," says Hanford. "Wrap your head around that."

"Give me ground zero," says Hoke.

Hoke punches at the empty space of radio.

"He's doing it again," says Jim. "Somebody shoot me fast."

"Ground zero, ground zero," raps Hoke. "Don't want to be no John Wayne hero, just me and Nero, jamming 'til it all burns down."

"Dated," says Jim.

"Like a train wreck," says Hanford.

"Fuck you guys," says Hoke.

They're early. They unload the equipment. They're melting. It's a heavily religious neighborhood with bilingual Jesus signs. Hanford goes looking for Froze Fruits. He comes back with what look like yogurt cups.

"Brooklyn Froze Fruits," says Hanford.

They inhale the stuff.

"Heard a good hospital joke yesterday," says Hoke.

"Yeah?" they say.

"Doctor says to his patient, 'I got some good news and some bad news.' So the guy, the patient, he says, 'Tell me the good news first, Doc.' The Doctor says, 'The good news is we found out you got twenty-four hours to live.' 'That's the good news? That's the fucking good news,' says the guy. 'What's the bad news?' So the Doc, he says, 'The bad news is I was supposed to tell you yesterday.' "

"Funny," says Hanford.

"Hardy, har," says Jim.

"My dad liked it," says Hoke. "He laughed."

"You ever think it's strange that when you get married all you ever see is your wife?" asks Hanford.

Hoke and Jim look at Hanford.

"Don't you ever get that feeling?"

"We're not married," says Hoke.

.

The auditorium has eight rows of orange vinyl-backed chairs, and blue tumbling mats line the floor. A barricade of extra chairs surrounds where the band will play. Hanford threads the chrome legs into his Fender Rhodes. Jim plugs his guitar into the amp. Hoke waits for Mikey to help him set up. It's Mikey's favorite part of the show.

"Need a name for this band," says Hoke.

"How about three guys doing anything not to play a top forty gig?" says Hanford.

"How about three guys looking for a captive audience?" says Jim.

Jim and Hanford look at Hoke.

"How about three sick fucks," says Hoke.

A social worker and two attendants herd the audience in. Half of them look like Federal Disaster Area people on Nightline, just stunned by the world, and the other half jerk along like over-wound windup toys. The three stubby girls that Hoke calls the Supremes. The kid with the helmet with an "I love Cape Canaveral" sticker on it. They call him John Glenn.

Jim's mother always said, "They're God's little mistakes." Jim's mother always said, "Don't stare."

Still no Mikey.

"I'm going to have to talk to that boy," says Hoke, and he sets up his drums and his mic on his own.

"Hello!" says Hoke.

They jerk their heads toward the speaker.

"Feeling a little caged and wild?" Hoke asks them.

"We gonna burn it up this morning?"

A few yells.

"You bet. One, two, one, two, three."

The music jump starts the Supremes right up out of their chairs. The girl in pink is always the leader. She leads them

95

in a one-two clap routine. The guy whose muscles have him tied in knots rolls across the tumbling mats. John Glenn goes rocketing past. God's little mistakes, thinks Jim. This one his Challenger, this one his Hindenburg, this one his World War Two.

"Feeling like an accident," sings Hoke. "Ever since I ran into you."

The apprentice drummer Hoke calls Ringo is glued on Hoke, watching his every move, keeping time, using one knee for a tom-tom, one knee for a snare, and his head for cymbal and bass. Hoke grins.

"Joe Cocker school of music," says Hoke.

"Wasn't like I wasn't looking," sings Hoke. "But you left me black and blue.

"Feeling like a sideswiped monk, baby you done turned me into junk."

They get about three claps.

"Thank you," says Hoke. "Good to be back. Been awhile."

Someone yells.

"Nothing we can do about it," says Hoke. "No funding, know what I mean? Talk to the government."

Drooling Freddy makes a run on the chair barrier.

"Freddy, stop," says the social worker.

Hoke gets to the barrier in time to push Freddy back.

Freddy says, "Hey, hey, hey."

"Freddy," says Hoke. "You seen Mikey?"

Freddy drools, shakes his head.

"Where's Mikey?" asks Hoke.

"Gone," says Freddy.

"Gone?" says Hoke. "Gone where?"

"Gone, gone, gone," says Freddy.

Hoke jumps the barricade and wades to the social worker who's social working as hard as she can.

Hanford and Jim play a little Old McDonald to keep their captive audience captive.

96

Hoke comes back over the barricade.

"What?" asks Jim.

Hoke walks right past Jim and sits back down behind his drums but doesn't pick up his drum sticks.

"Florida," says Hoke. "They sent him to Florida for Christ's sake."

"What?" asks Hanford.

The audience is getting antsy. Freddy makes another run on the chair barricade and is halfway over it before an attendant drags him back.

"Think maybe we ought to start again?" asks Jim.

Hoke looks at Jim.

"Maybe I should start us again," Jim says.

Hanford and Jim play the "Wash Song" with no help from Hoke. The social worker stands up this little guy that's wearing a pair of jeans cuffed to the knees, as if Mom and Dad are still expecting him to grow into normal. Jim sings.

"Baby took me to the laundry mat, put me in with the blues."

They play their institutional version. It runs about twenty minutes. Jim keeps glancing back at Hoke who just stares off into his snare.

"You permanent pressed me, you permanent messed me, then you were through."

Lots of hooting and hollering from the crowd, then a rat-a-tat-tat of drums. Jim looks back at Hoke. He's holding his sticks again.

"You okay?" Jim asks.

"A-okay," says Hoke.

Hoke leans into his mic.

"Like to introduce the band," says Hoke. "On keyboards, a good argument for not flying the friendly skies, Mister Otis Redding."

Hanford looks at Jim.

"Humor him," Jim says.

Hanny wow-wows the Fender Rhodes.

"O-tis," says Hoke.

"On guitar, Mister Just Didn't Say No, Jimmy Hendrixs."

Jim slaps his Stratocaster, hoping Jimmy in the sky isn't listening.

"Last is me," says Hoke, and he does another rat-a-tat-tat. "I'm Hoke."

The girl in the pink dress reaches across the chairs.

"What's your name little girl?" asks Hoke.

She plays peek-a-boo behind her stubby hands.

"Kelly!" says Hoke. "Kelly, do you have a favorite song you want us to play?"

Kelly swings her head wildly one way and then the other.

"No," says Hoke. "No?"

"Okay," Hoke says.

"Any of you out there got girl friends?" asks Hoke.

Yelling.

"How about boy friends?" asks Hoke.

They yell some more.

"Well this one's for all you lovers," says Hoke.

"Sticky Lips," Hoke says to Hanford and Jim. "And volume."

They hit it.

"I'm sticky, sticky, sticky, sticky for you," sings Hoke.

A dance tune. The whole room is rocking. A woman with orange shorts and white whale legs starts doing a cheer-leader routine. The two attendants can't keep themselves sitting any longer. They're up and boogieing.

"Soul train," says Hoke.

The Supremes are getting out of sync. Ringo pounds himself on the head.

This could be our own Titanic, thinks Jim, and we're the band going down with the ship.

Hanford looks ready to head for the life boats, forget the women and children.

"The way you move your hips, gives me sticky lips, sticky my lips . . . "

They lose Hanford. Jim turns to see him pointing at a kid in the back who is wailing on this old guy in a wheelchair, beating the hell out of him.

"Sticky for you, sticky for you, sticky for you . . . "

One of the boogieing attendants finally notices and tackles the kid, drags him thrashing from the room on the last refrain.

Meltdown.

The social worker is headed the band's way, arms waving over her head as if she were trying to stop a train headed for a bus load of kids stalled on the tracks.

Think this gig is over, thinks Jim.

"Hoke," Jim says.

"Time for one more," says Hoke. "Any requests?"

"Don't," says the social worker. "Don't, don't, don't."

"Don't know that one," says Hoke.

"Beirut Boogie," says Hoke to Hanford and Jim.

Jim is thinking this might be a mistake.

"Anybody out there know how to break dance?" Hoke asks them.

Do they know how to break dance? When Hoke whams his tom-tom half of them dive straight on their faces. Definitely a mistake.

"You got hostage on my heart, you're tearing me apart, you Beiruted me."

Jim thinks he could be inside an overheated atom a chemistry teacher once tried to explain to him. Screaming somethings whiz by like electrons, jumping orbits, jumping barricades, jumping everything in between.

"Car bomb your face, mess you up all over the place."

"Cuffed at the Knees" bounces away like a runaway pogo stick. Their cheerleader goes into a high kick routine. She kicks Freddy in the head. Down goes Freddy. Down come Hanford's shades. John Glenn ricochets off all four walls. The guy whose muscles have him tied in knots rolls across the floor, knocking over Supremes like bowling pins. The social worker is stuck straddling the barricade, the tops of her panty hose showing.

Hoke beats his cymbal, kicks his bass, avalanches sound over them. Half the room whams with him. Ringo overheats and flops on the floor like a hooked fish in a boat bottom. Hoke blows out a stick. He keeps pounding with the good one and the splinter. He's eating his skins up, playing his ass off, as if this were the Garden or something. And then a stumble.

Jim has visions of a hurdler catching his foot, going down, slow motion. Stumble-catch-stumble, then the drums fall off all together.

There is a big wide open silence. Like all the water drained from an ocean. Then it washes back in on them, barking, braying, mooing, it sounds like a barnyard. Hoke holds two broken sticks, his head hanging between his shoulders.

Jim looks at Hanford. Hanford looks at Jim. Jim unslings his guitar and walks back to Hoke.

"Hey," Jim says.

Hoke looks up. Streams are streaming down his face.

"Florida," says Hoke. "They send the guy to fucking Florida without telling anybody. What kind of shit is that?"

Hoke drops Jim last. Jim opens the station wagon door but doesn't get out.

"Wasn't about Mikey so much," says Hoke. "Mostly it wasn't."

"Yeah," says Jim.

"Yesterday," Hoke says. "Yesterday was kind of rough."

They watch traffic.

Finally Jim says, "Better jump."

He steps back out into the soup. Hoke guns the wagon away from the curb.

"Hey," yells Jim.

Hoke stops. Jim is in the street, dodging cars.

"The good news is they didn't nuke Manhattan."

"That's the good news?" says Hoke.

Pilot Flying Cover

Pɪʟᴏᴛ ɪѕ ɪɴ ᴀ ʜᴏʟᴅɪɴɢ ᴘᴀᴛᴛᴇʀɴ over Kensington. He banks wide over the cricket pitch and Farmer Will's garden, loops the horse barn, the baseball diamond, the runway, Snugglebunny, and Farmer Will's garden again, crosses the empty creek bed, kicking up sand, and then pulls into a steep climb to clear the hill and the cafeteria and the dormitories. He thinks he has a hydraulic leak and he's using all his fuel in case he has to make a belly landing. When his gauges read empty he lines up on final with the basketball court. He has STOL capabilities so when he finds his gear is solid and he doesn't have to worry about ground-looping, he cuts his rollout at mid-court.

It's hot like it only gets hot in a Texas Indian summer. The asphalt is chewed-bubble gum soft and sticks to Pilot's shoes which pop with each step he takes. He taxies over to Katie's laid out light pole that she uses for thinking, shuts down his engines, and leans back on the steel reinforced concrete to think himself. He tries to sit right where Katie sits, because it seems to make her smarter. Katie. Beautiful and as close to a swing-wing F-111 as any girl Pilot has ever met or seen a picture of. He stares off into the big blue.

Pilot is leaning on the concrete he doesn't know how long when he notices the blue going to black too fast. He sits up and sees clouds barreling across the prairie, low and dark and solid as stone. When he gets to his feet the gusts stretch him out like a windsock. He makes a carrier take-off, all afterburner and blue flame, and is headed for shelter when he notices Farmer Will still in his garden. Pilot peels off and dives, skims the cricket pitch to where Farmer Will digs like crazy, as if he were building a dike against the storm.

"Will," says Pilot. "We better get out of here."

Farmer Will doesn't pay Pilot any mind. Pilot circles the garden, side-slipping, watching the black rain curtain close in.

"We're gonna get wet," says Pilot.

Then a lightning bolt welds the horizon, and the ground thudding thunder bounces Farmer Will right out of his garden and next to Pilot, straining for the altitude they need to make the hill. As they charge over the hilltop they hear the howl of the Kensington air horn that Neville Pitney uses to scare them underground during tornado weather. They don't beat the rain.

The cafeteria basement could be a London air raid shelter; kids mill aimlessly with pillows and blankets, as if they're just realizing that their houses and parents were blown to bits, and there is nothing left to go home to. Bucky yells for everyone to be quiet so he can get a head count. Pilot puts himself on automatic pilot, and only takes the controls when collision is imminent.

"Christ Pilot, would you stop running around in circles," says Bucky. "I'm trying to count."

Pilot picks up Essie the librarian on his tail and works to shake her but she won't shake. She just plows along behind him, no grace and a brick in the air. It's fun for awhile, letting her close on him and listening to her wheeze and threat. But finally he gets tired and does a half-loop-one-eighty-coming-back, firing missiles and cannons to finish this business.

"Tuffffff, tuffffff, braap, braap, braap."

Essie the librarian squawks, breaks off, trailing smoke and fire, breaking up midair. Pilot does a victory roll. He's painting a kill-flag beneath his canopy when someone collars him from behind.

"Pilot," says Katie. "You seen Dexter?"

She gives him a Pearl Harbor in his heart.

"No," says Pilot.

"Help me find Dexter," says Katie.

If Katie asked Pilot to jump without a parachute he would.

He makes a recon run around the room. Katie once told Pilot that Dexter was something to see during a tornado. The Kensington air horn reminds him of the noise his guns made when he zap-zapped the shit out of whatever it was he zapped the shit out of, and his eyes get wide. Dexter's plane was called a Dragon Ship, the same as a DC-3 except that mounted in the cargo compartment it had three mini-guns that could fire six thousand rounds a minute. The pilot of a Dragon Ship flew at night, using an infrared sight mounted over his left shoulder to mark targets on the ground. When he pressed a button it was as if he had turned on a garden hose of bullets, a dragon's fiery breath.

Bucky makes a reach for Pilot.

"Braap, braap."

Pilot hits the afterburners, smokes it out into the crowd. Dexter still hasn't shown, so Pilot lands himself next to Katie. The wind is howling upstairs.

"No Dexter," says Pilot.

"Wait," says Katie.

She's listening to the television. The weather man says there is a tornado watch for Crockett County until midnight, and that the Crockett Fire Chief saw a tornado south of town. That is where Kensington is, south of town.

"Dexter's outside," says Katie. "We have to find him, maybe he's not all right."

"Okay," says Pilot.

Bucky is blocking their way.

"Nobody goes upstairs until Mr. Pitney gives the all clear," says Bucky.

They back off.

"Napalm is what he wants," says Pilot. "I'll blow him to shit with a cluster of black and yellow, oil and flame flowers."

Katie grabs Pilot by the arm and drags him away.

"Where's Will?" asks Katie.

They find Farmer Will and huddle up.

"We have to find Dexter," says Katie to Farmer Will. "If we all make a run for it, Bucky can't get us all."

Farmer Will nods.

"Are you with us?" asks Katie.

Farmer Will nods again.

"Okay," says Pilot. "Let's go."

Bucky doesn't see them coming until they are on him and past him and climbing the stairs. Pilot is in the middle, lifting his knees high, with Katie on his right and Farmer on his left. They have almost made the upstairs landing when he hears the pursuit closing in. And then Katie disappears and Pilot turns to see that Bucky is pulling her back down the stairs by her ankles, looking as if he is drowning her, looking as if he is pulling her under. Pilot reaches for Katie. Here comes Neville Pitney and more teachers.

"Go," says Katie. "Go, go, go."

They free-fall out into the storm, Farmer Will and Pilot. The wind hits them like a hand slap. It blows the whole world horizontal.

"Meet me at the dorm walk," says Pilot, and they go searching their separate ways.

It's raining India-monsoon hard on Pilot's head. He checks

Dexter's apartment and the teachers' lounge and Physics and the auditorium but Dexter isn't anywhere. He checks the three old quonsets and then circles back to the dorm walk and waits for Farmer Will, holding on to the step railing so that he won't get blown away.

Farmer Will gallops his lanky gallop out of the storm, waving and pointing.

"What?" asks Pilot. "What?"

Pilot follows Farmer Will to the wheelchair tracks on the grass and dirt saddle that leads to where the hillside drops away. The tracks follow the drop over the edge and Pilot and Farmer Will dive after them. Lightning explodes around their heads, muffled by clouds that sink toward the prairie like squid ink spreading on an ocean bottom.

The wheelchair tracks disappear into the creek which is running over the top of the bridge.

"I hope the water didn't take him," says Pilot.

Farmer Will isn't bothered by the water and he starts across the bridge, feeling ahead with his feet. Pilot slips once and the water grabs at his waist, but Farmer Will reaches for him and pulls him across. The way Will is fearless about the water makes Pilot think he must have been a lifeguard or maybe a fish before.

On the cricket pitch the wheelchair tracks are filled with rain and look like little canals. Pilot and Farmer Will follow the canals to where they empty out on to the old cement of the runway. Now they can't tell which way Dexter went and Pilot is wishing for Katie and her lamp pole so he could think better. The rain is sideways and stinging his face. Farmer Will ducks to the ground and digs at the wet red dirt, feeding it to his mouth as fast as he can.

"Snugglebunny," says Pilot.

Pilot firewalls his throttles and takes off running. Farmer Will trails along beside him, his wingman, skirting the edge of the strip. The wind tosses them, once dropping Pilot to his knees, but even with aching lungs he doesn't let up.

They reach the end of the runway and are lost until Farmer Will points out Dexter's chair. It's up to its rims in the prairie mud, but no Dexter. A monster lightning flash lights up the whole sky and rocks them back on their heels. Pilot sees a big snake-track furrow, the mark Dexter's body left as he dragged it across the field. Dexter's hands have left dents in the earth. Three different funnels are reaching for the ground.

"Let's go," says Pilot.

Farmer Will is strobed by the lightning, frozen by the spinning clouds, and Pilot has to yank him to get him moving again.

Snugglebunny looms out of the storm like a ghost ship. Her skin is dull-rusted and she disappears from them between lightning flashes. The rain beats against the metal so hard that it sounds as if pistons are still pounding inside the rusty cowlings. Wind buffets the plane and it seems to Pilot as if Snugglebunny is straining against herself and all the years and is about to jump into the sky.

The belly hatch is hanging broken-jaw open. Pilot swings up into the fuselage and pulls Farmer Will in behind him. They are soaked and shivering and Pilot has to hold himself to stop shaking. He watches Farmer Will's silhouette quiver as he sniffs the musty air. The smell of Snugglebunny is the smell of twenty-five years of Kensington students grabbing at themselves and each other.

Pilot follows a trail of mud to the cockpit. Dexter is in the pilot's seat.

"Who's that?" asks Dexter.

"Pilot, Pilot and Farmer Will," says Pilot.

Dexter doesn't say anything but just keeps staring out the port side of the plane, as if he can see something. Rain pounds off the glass, sheeting it. Dexter is covered in mud and bleeding from somewhere. Pilot gets a closer look at Dexter's face and sees that his left eye is twitching so hard that Pilot wonders if it might not seize-up on him.

"I am Puff," says Dexter.

Dexter sways back and forth and holds on to the control column as the gusts push at the ailerons and elevators. Snugglebunny begins to vibrate as the wind feels at the old metal and tries to lift it from the ground.

"There's some tornados outside," says Pilot to Dexter.

That doesn't seem to get anywhere near Dexter.

"I can disappear anybody," says Dexter.

Dexter is far away in a war, and Pilot doesn't know how to get him back or even if he wants to come back. He's wide-eyed and the way he's straining against the controls you would think their lives depended on it. The storm shifts the plane a little and Farmer Will starts scratching at the floor. He scampers back to the belly hatch to see about getting closer to the ground, but after a look outside he changes his mind. Dexter locks his arms and starts shaking as if he is going into a stall.

"We're going down," says Dexter.

"What do we do?" Pilot asks him.

Dexter is sagging.

"Puff's tired," says Dexter. "Puff's got no legs."

Pilot drops into the cracked leather of the copilot's seat and waits to see if that will throw Dexter off balance, but Dexter doesn't seem to notice. He's fighting the controls, and seems to be losing. The storm quiets for a moment, and then the wind that has been pushing on Snugglebunny finally figures out the right leverage. They are scooting toward the runway, sideways, either in a tornado or flying wingman to it. The whole plane comes off the ground as it goes bouncing along, trying to get into the air. Pilot feels the landing gear give, and then the metal of the bottom of the plane hits the cement of the runway and starts tearing apart. Above that Pilot hears a sound he has never heard before, and he turns to see where it is coming from. It's coming from Farmer Will's throat and it starts like the first cough of a volcano and then grows into a howl that seems to come from underneath them, from deep inside the earth. Dirt flecks Farmer Will's teeth and mud oozes from both corners of his mouth. Dexter turns to Pilot, his face twisted and sideways.

"You take over," says Dexter.

Pilot grabs the control column in front of him and then sees Dexter's hands and forearms reach up and take Farmer Will by the neck and start to crush him. Pilot is sure Dexter is going to kill Will and he stops flying and starts looking for something to hit Dexter on the head with. There is nothing in the cockpit and Pilot is about to head aft when Farmer Will's screams turn to something else, and Pilot realizes that Dexter is not doing anything but holding Will.

Pilot grabs the yoke and goes back to flying, but the tornado has left them behind. Snugglebunny is back on the ground. The yoke kicks softly in Pilot's hands, the last flutters of a dying bird, and then the wind dies off all together. In light from flashes of far off lightning, Pilot sees that the guns are gone from Dexter's eyes. Pilot drops the yoke and lifts his feet from the rudder pedals. Soon the beating rain has him gone from Texas.

Pilot comes awake in a quiet, the sun barely out of the ground. Dexter is asleep in the pilot's seat. Pilot walks back through the fuselage, but Will isn't there either. The belly hatch is mashed closed so Pilot sticks his head out the starboard gunner's port. Snugglebunny is on the edge of the runway, about halfway from the end, and Dexter's wheelchair is sitting next to the wing. The mud has been cleaned from the wheelchair and it reflects the long morning light. Pilot drops out of the gunner's port and walks around the tail of the plane. Farmer Will is on the edge of the strip, smiling and chomping on his dirt.

"Morning, Will," says Pilot.

Farmer Will smiles big and offers Pilot a wet clod. Pilot squats down next to him and takes a bite of it as if it were an apple. He tries to swallow but it's all grit and he ends up spitting it out.

"I don't know how you eat that shit," says Pilot.

When Katie finds them, the Indian summer heat is boiling up so much steam off the runway that Snugglebunny looks as if she is topping out at twenty thousand. Pilot is on Snugglebunny's wing, his back up against the cowling of the number three engine. Katie is wet to the knees. She sees Dexter's empty wheelchair.

"Did you find him?"

"He's in the plane," says Pilot. "Sleeping."

Katie circles the wing, splashes through a water pool on the runway, and disappears into the starboard gunner's port.

Pilot tilts his head back, breathes in the faintest smell of old engine oil and maybe gasoline. Across the cricket pitch Farmer Will looks to be hoeing the top of a cloud.

Katie drops to the runway. She takes her shoes and socks off, then wrings the corners of her jeans. She lays her socks out on the wing metal, climbs barefoot up on to the wing, and walks past Pilot and out to the end.

"Jesus Pilot, I thought you guys were dead," says Katie.

"Me too," says Pilot.

Katie's tracks evaporate off the wing one by one. The sun burns through the last of the ground fog to an earth broomed clean by tornados. It's flying weather. Farmer Will is in his garden doing his garden things, Snugglebunny is taking Dexter to where he goes in his sleep, barefoot Katie is wing walking, and Pilot is flying cover.

"Let the Babies
Keep Their Hearts"

I HUNKER IN THE ALFALFA, in the shade of my split-axle dump truck, in a daydream that's all tropical downpours. I'm chewing at a stalk of volunteer barley, working up spit enough so I won't choke myself to death on the dust Harold kicks up every time he swings by. It's bone dry out here, and if it weren't for center pivots this crappy land would be dead. I can't believe the idiot farmer who's having us take a third cutting off the pitiful stuff. It's like taking part in a massacre. No way it'll make it through winter.

Harold is making one last sweep with his excuse for a hay swather, an old nameless thing he's dragging with a yellow John Deere, and it comes to me that nothing looks stupider than a yellow John Deere. When he shuts down I gun my truck under the unloading chute of his hopper. Harold's wearing a pair of goggles and a red bandanna and looks like a lost tank commander. He takes off the goggles and looks at me, his face twisted up the way it gets when he's been thinking.

"I don't understand how they can kill babies and take the hearts out of them just so's they can save a baboon," is what Harold finally says.

It takes me about two beats to figure this out. Harold's been reading Newsweek again, and as per usual he's got the story all ass-backwards.

"It's probably not just any baboon," I say, thinking Jesus will kill me for this one. "It's probably a space baboon or a special smart one they're saving."

"But killing babies," says Harold. "I mean whose babies are they?"

"Sure they're not regular babies," I say. "They must be brain dead already, or sick, or maybe they aren't even American."

I leave Harold worrying about his heart-robbed babies and hook it for the mill. It's my last run of the day and I'm feeling a little ragged. Great Western operates seven days a week, twenty-four hours a day, and we drivers work twelve-hour shifts. Every two weeks we switch from days to nights or vice-versa, and put in an eighteen-hour swing. Tomorrow I'm swinging from days to nights. There must be something illegal about it; I keep going to sleep at the wheel and ending up in cornfields and irrigation ditches. The mill only shuts down when it rains, and it's been blue skies since the day we started cutting. Spend the best part of my brains wishing for a monsoon.

I wheel into the mill yard, back the truck up to the dumping bin, leave the dumping to Mike, who works my opposite shift and shares my truck, and head for the truck barn to punch out. The truck barn has two work bays, a wall full of tools, a workbench, a coffeepot, a time clock, our time cards, and a "Number of Days Without an Accident" sign which is in double digits for the first time this summer.

Gus is at the workbench, making coffee, but he's forgotten to put the pot underneath the filter and the coffee is streaming down on the hot plate, hissing and steaming, and spilling to the floor.

"Shit, shit, shit," says Gus, running one way and then the other, grabbing for something to catch the coffee with. This is not atypical Great Western driver behavior.

"Good thing you aren't an airline pilot," I say.

The only way to stay alive around this place is to inhale speed, legal or otherwise, and right now Gus looks to be operating about thirty feet off the ground. My own hands started shaking the Fourth of July.

"Shit, shit, shit," says Gus, burning himself as he sticks an oil drip pan underneath the streaming coffee.

I punch out and head for Fort Collins, taking Highway Fourteen so I won't have to pass the sheep feedlots. Fourteen is not the fastest way but there's nothing in the world that smells worse to me than sheep shit. I'd rather eat a cow shit sandwich than step in sheep shit with my work boots on.

Take the back door through town, vault the railroad tracks, and pass the gherkin factory. A guy once fell into the vats and they didn't find him for ten years. They looked all over for him and finally decided he'd left his wife, run off with another woman. Nobody imagined he was getting pickled for life.

I stop at Avogadro's Number for a #4 GobbleyGook, which is what happens to a turkey if he walks through a kitchen combine and gets lettuce and mayo tossed on him. I used to eat here when I went to college one time. I lived on the third floor of a high rise dormitory and we called ourselves the Pukes. We even had a Puke cheer. This one dumb shit Ag major went to a party on the tenth floor and tilted his beer back too far and fell out the window. That's about all I remember.

I down my sandwich and head west toward Rist Canyon. Sue Ellen, my sometimes girlfriend, and Melinda own a little horse-riding ranch ten miles up and they rent me their used-to-be potato barn for fifty dollars a month. That includes sharing the bathroom and the kitchen in the main house. I'm still not sure who's getting the better end of the deal. The Rist is a little canyon I would've called a gulch. Following the curves in the road I move in and out of shadows, and with my window open I feel that the darker air is already cold. This summer's been so dry that after the melt was gone the creek just altogether disappeared. All that's left are these lonely-looking round stones.

The girls have stereo speakers strung out to the barn and Willie yelling up the canyon. Couple of tough guys these girls. They're in the corral with Bo and Blackie, circled around a fire. Bo is Melinda's black lab, and Blackie is an albino Shetland pony. They're about halfway through a case of Buckhorns, which tells you something about the slimness of the horse-riding business.

"Well if it ain't old Manual Labor," says Sue Ellen.

Sue Ellen is blonde as California, has boy-shoulders, and has shit-kickers on the end of her Baja California legs. I give her a kiss.

"Hey," says Melinda.

"Don't say that word," I say.

I sit in the dirt and lean back against the corral wood.

"Man alive," I say. "This is a hurting pup you're looking at."

"You ought to quit that job," says Melinda. "You're working yourself to death."

I call her Muy Linda in my heart. She's a barrel racer, a calf roper, a mountain climber of El Capitan forwards and backwards, and she's got the most beautiful scarred kneecaps you've ever seen. I don't know, maybe it's my own kneecaps as a boy that I'm after, but when she wears those knee-ragged jeans, and I see those white scars, God Jesus. I shouldn't be thinking like this.

She throws me a Buckhorn.

"Drink," she says.

The sun crashes into the Mummy range and Melinda grabs a rotten ponderosa pine fence post and throws it on the fire. The wind is blowing from the Divide so we sit together on the west side of the corral to keep the smoke out of our faces. We finish the Buckhorns and Melinda digs for some Mad Dog.

"No sir," I say. "This kid's driving a swing shift tomorrow."

"Manual, Manual," says Sue Ellen. "Tomorrow's tomorrow."

That Mad Dog gets us elevated. We crank the music and start dancing like wild horses. I dance with Bo, and Sue Ellen tries to ride Blackie. Melinda is flamed-up and when the radio comes out with a grinding beat she starts shaking her hips and circling the fire.

"Do us a rain dance," I say.

Melinda tears her shirt off so fast that a button pops to the dust. Bo and I stop to watch. She holds her arms way out from her body and moves them back and forth like a Tahiti woman, her leg and arm bone shadows doing a broken puppet dance on the corral railings. Her bra is black and it barely holds her in as she shimmies and kicks up dirt. Sue Ellen stomps beer cans and I Yahoo, but when Melinda takes her bra off I say to myself, Pedro, you better sit down. She has this tiny waist that her jeans barely grab on to, and you can see her bottom three sets of ribs perfectly. Above that it's just acres of Annapurnas, Kilimanjaros, and K-2's which she shakes for me and Sue Ellen and Bo and Blackie and all the stars in the sky.

"If that don't make it rain," I say. "It ain't raining."

"Why didn't y'all join me?" says Melinda, getting cold pretty quick and getting her shirt back on.

" 'Cause I don't got nothing like you do," says Sue Ellen.

She's right about that. I'm a witness. Her chest looks like it's been gone over three times with a tandem field plane.

"I don't have nothing either," I say.

We make pillows out of feed sacks and say we're going to watch for shooting stars. It takes about thirty seconds for a big monster one to go plowing past.

"Make a wish, make a wish," says Melinda.

"I'm wishing for a gully washer," I say. "I'm wishing for one telephone call to God, I'll say, Jack, time to drowned the world again. Forty days and forty nights and then some."

"I'm wishing for a Marlboro man," says Melinda. "Some guy to come by so I can tie him up and talk French to him."

God Jesus.

"I wish I had tits like Melinda," says Sue Ellen. "But we got to wait for another star 'cause if you say your wish out loud it doesn't count."

When I wake up the fire is cold. Melinda comes around but Sue Ellen is dead to the world.

"Who's going to carry her?" I ask.

"She's your girlfriend."

Sue Ellen won't let go of her feed-sack pillow. I put her over my shoulder.

"Help, my back," I say. "This girl's all choice."

Melinda holds open the doors. I hear Sue Ellen's head smack against something on the way through the kitchen and then I drop her on her bed, feed sack and all. When I turn around Melinda already has her shirt off again.

I feel like I'm thinking with some kind of extinct dinosaur brain. Don't sleep with the help? That's not it. Don't sleep with the landlord? That might be it. Don't sleep with your sometimes girlfriend's best girlfriend? That's it. She drops her pants and I see those kneecaps.

"I'm going to bed," says Melinda. "You think it's too cold, you can stay the night in the house."

If I think it's too cold?

When my Timex Triathlon watch alarm goes wa, wa, wa, I think maybe somebody's let a kicking mule loose inside of my head. It keeps on wa, wa-ing and I think that that's what I get for living up a canyon with screaming mountain women. On about the last three wa, wa, wa's I put together that I'm not in my potato barn, that I'm not in my bed, and that I'm not in Sue Ellen's bed either. Oh shit. I open my eyes. This doesn't look familiar. This is a most unfamiliar landscape. Then I realize I'm face to kneecaps with the most beautiful kneecaps in the world. Oh shit. Oh shit. I don't even want to right myself to get the big picture but I do. Oh shit, oh shit, oh shit. Melinda's naked but for her boots.

I cover the evidence with a blanket, lift the blanket for one last look, God Jesus, dive into my jeans which are green and stiff with alfalfa juice, and bang into about four walls stumbling for the bathroom. When I turn the light on I wish I hadn't. I see Sue Ellen's black stockings strung over the shower curtain like dead king snakes, I see her panties and bras hanging on the drying line like shot and skinned animals, and then I see me.

I wash myself from the armpits up, on the way through the kitchen grab a packet of Instant Breakfast, and when I stumble outside I nearly brown in my green pants.

"Yikes," I say.

Standing right at the back door, blowing big puffs of steam from each nostril, is Blackie looking like a midget horse-ghost.

"Here I slave my guts out for the likes of you," I say. "And for thanks you scare the shit out of me?"

It's nine thousand degrees below zero and my hair nearly freezes in the fifty feet between the house and my truck. I jump the truck into reverse and I'm doing about five miles an hour when I ka-whamo the shit out of something. Shit, shit, shit.

I get out to look. It's still too dark to see. It's Sue Ellen's Toyota. I feel with my hand along the side of the Toyota to know what's happened. Just behind the front wheel well I've pushed in the body metal a good six inches. For about one trillionth of a second I consider telling her, but then my better judgement kicks in. No reason to ruin her day before the sun is up. No reason to end my life either.

At the bottom of the Rist, out of the canyon shadow, the road rises hard to the left where I once dumped my bike when I was in high school. This girl I was in love with was on the back. She burned the shit out of her leg on the muffler. It was springtime. Got caught in some sand left over from winter. Every time I see her she brings up her opinion that I ruined her chances for Miss Colorado, Miss America, and beyond. I left some skin on this corner myself.

One look at the sky tells me Melinda's rain dance didn't do any good. Not my wishing either. I turn south and swing past Horsetooth to check the water. I heard on the radio-news that the level's the lowest it's been since they built the dam. The long narrow gleam coming off the reservoir hurts my head. Some guy was once waterskiing and he skied right through a ball of rattlesnakes. He was dead before he got wet.

I pull into the mill yard, park, and carefully put my one foot in front of the other one over to the truck barn, heading for the coffee.

"You chasing parked cars?" asks Mike.

I'm concentrating on making my hands pour a cup of coffee. I shake the battalion-sized bottle of aspirin over the mug until I count enough splashes that I think it might help.

"How about the new Newsweek?" asks Mike.

Beginning of summer I got a subscription to Newsweek to

celebrate getting my job. I keep them stashed under the driver's seat so I'll have something to read if the mower breaks or if the mill shuts in. Mike didn't associate with me for all of June just 'cause I was reading Newsweek. Then he started reading it himself.

I try to answer him, tell him to go away already or something, but it turns out that my mouth isn't working yet. I've still got half a dry Instant Breakfast stuck in my throat.

"I read that last one four times," says Mike.

I look at the mug I'm drinking out of. It says on it, Kiss me, I'm confused. Un-huh.

Feeling like I'm in some pretty thick ground fog, I check the air in the tires and put a couple quarts of oil in the engine. It's lousy death-for-sure equipment they got us driving, so I do everything I can in the way of preventative maintenance. Gus comes staggering in looking for his truck too. There's three of us driving trucks on each shift to keep a steady flow of hay arriving at the mill. Working my shift driving trucks are Gus and Chet, and goombay Harold is out in the field on the tractor. Harold's only been with us a month. He hired on after some other tractor-driving Harold stuck his hand in the mower's chopping box without disconnecting the PTO. When the stone he was trying to unstick came unstuck, the blades started turning again. I'm sure glad I wasn't there to see that mess.

When I get to the field Harold is already waiting with a load. He climbs up in the cab to get out of the chill and I pour him a cup of coffee.

"Gosh I hope not," says Harold.

"Gosh I hope not what?" I ask.

"Gosh I hope they aren't taking the hearts out of just any old baby."

This, I figure out, is more of yesterday's conversation.

"Don't you ever talk to anybody at home?" I ask.

■

Operating close to brain-dead across the morning, I try to hyperventilate myself to stay conscious and out of the bar ditches. I keep getting last night flashbacks that land on my brain like bricks. I try to chase'em from my head before I see anything bad, but it's ugly. There's me kissing and declaring eternal love to a pair of kneecaps; there's me saying, Let's play mountain climbing, you're Mount Everest, and my lips are Sir Edmund Percival Hillary and his faithful Sherpa Tenzing; there's me saying, Sherpa Tenzing, help me, help me, oxygen, I think I got a case of high altitude sickness; there's me saying, Oh, no, Sir Edmund, it appears we have ascended the wrong massif, look at that other one, it's taller, we got to do it all over; there's me again saying, Sure, when Melinda asks if she should get her lariat so we can really rodeo. There's her saying, One guy used to take down the bull by biting him on the lip. There's a demonstration of that. It gets worse. Be lucky not to come out of this a steer.

When I'm making what seems like about my twenty millionth run, I see another bird-shit yellow truck coming the other way. Whenever Gus and I pass each other on the road we play a game of halfhearted chicken to wake ourselves. At four telephone poles we cross into each other's lane, and at two telephone poles we cross back. This time I switch lanes no problem and so does Gus. Then I cross back. Now we're closing at about one hundred twenty-five and Gus is not moving back. At one telephone pole his truck starts crabbing for the other side but it looks highly unlikely to me that it will make it. Gus's bugged out eyes are getting closer and closer and I'm wishing for a seat belt. With a six foot drop running both sides of the road I bury my brakes and get ready for dead. This will solve a lot of problems. The last thing I see before I close my eyes is my own scared-shitless reflection in Gus's windshield, and then our mirrors tick.

At the mill I go shaky-legged looking for Joe Bill, our occasional foreman. I find him cleaning out the gravel screens. Joe Bill pretty much put the ug in ugly. He's got tobacco stained baby teeth, he's round as a barrel, and on his feet he has these little itty-bitty Nocona boots that don't look like they could give him any kind of balance.

"Say," I say. "You wouldn't happen to know if this Gus is trying to kill himself, would you?"

"Why?" says Joe Bill.

"That pud-knocker just about head-oned me," I say.

"Every one of you idiots deserves to get killed dead," says Joe Bill.

Gus comes wheeling back into the yard and parks alongside the truck barn. I take a long mean look at him but he looks too sick to be mad at. He's all white in the face and looking like he wants to puke. I wait for him to get out of his truck but he doesn't so I walk over.

"You not feeling too good?" I ask.

"We almost nearly got killed," says Gus.

"Telling me, you dumb bastard," I say.

Gus gets out of his truck and wobbles toward his front tire. He used to be a pretty good basketball player until he got thrown off the team for drinking. He's got no touch for the ball anymore and all he has left are these mile long arms and legs that get in the way of everything he does, like walking.

"I was taking a load of pellets to the feed store," says Gus. "I never done that with a load of pellets. I had nine tons on the bed and she wouldn't come back."

I start feeling a little queasy myself when I get what Gus is talking about. A load of fresh alfalfa only weighs a couple of tons, and seven more tons makes a whole lot of steering difference.

"Guess we better not do that anymore," I say.

"Not me, un-uh, not me," says Gus, and then he wobbles off toward the toilet, probably to clean out his shorts.

∎

The mill backed up while they cleaned the gravel screens so we're doing the sitting and waiting routine. We have Big Gulp Dr. Peppers for lunch and then Chet takes the Bobcat out in the mill yard and starts popping wheelies. He raises the scoop halfway and takes off in reverse and then jams it into forward. The machine momentarily looks like it's back-flipping, then it charges for about twenty feet before the front whomps down. Gus has revived himself and is throwing clods at Chet and the clods smack against the wire protection screen and spatter.

"It's Front-end Loader Man," shouts Chet. "He's invincible."

I pick up a clod and heave it, and as it leaves my hand Chet spins the cat around and I know he's in trouble. That clod goes right between the screens and straight for his face like a homing missile. Chet has the control levers locked and is laying down donuts in the gravel and bleeding pretty good by the time Gus and I get to him. We chase around trying to get him to stop. Finally I hit the kill switch and the motor sputters out. Chet looks at me funny from beneath his N-Serve farmers' cap.

"I think I might of broke your nose, Chet," I say.

Nothing's getting through to Chet and he's happy to just stay sitting. Then I see Joe Bill come out of the office and I wish I wasn't where I am.

"Chet broke his nose," I say.

"You fighting?" asks Joe Bill.

"He got hit with a dirt clod."

"Who did it?"

"Didn't mean to," I say. "You want me to take him to the hospital?"

Joe Bill gets old Chet out of the Bobcat and leads him across the yard like a lost dog.

"Sorry, Chet," I say.

"You two morons get back to driving," says Joe Bill.

We watch them leave.

"Don't worry," Gus says. "Joe Bill's just pissed 'cause he'll have to change the 'Number of Days Without an Accident' sign back to zero."

The monster long afternoon stretches out in front of me on a shimmering two lane of asphalt that seems to go on and on out into the middle of some death valley where it disappears into heat waves. I just keep telling myself that we're putting the bread on the table, that we're an essential cog in the great American food factory. That's only a good argument when you're too wired to remember that people don't eat alfalfa pellets, and cows don't eat alfalfa pellets; it's horses we're risking our lives for, Blackie and her friends. I try not to think about it when my feet are anywhere near the ground.

For what feels like about a year there aren't any shadows, the sun so bright that it beats right through everything, including the roof of the truck, banging on my head. My whole body sticks to the black plastic seat. I get a crick in my neck from looking over my shoulder for a dented Toyota assassin vehicle that I keep imagining is following me. Finally the light stretches out longer, and then I'm chasing a big truck shadow when I'm going east to the field, and frying my eyes out when I'm going west to the mill. And then the sun goes down and I say, Thank-you-Lord because that means there's only four hours to go before this day's done.

The air cools off fast, dropping into gullies and depressions in the land. In the field I park on hilltops of warmth. When I'm waiting to dump a load at the mill I stand next to the dryer. It's a big cylinder about ten feet across and has something like a Saturn Five rocket engine strapped on one end. The flames go shooting through the cylinder where the wet hay is and dry it out. The inside of the cylinder is fluted so that the hay moves away from the flames and finally is dumped out dry at the other end. Then it gets crushed into powder and compacted into pellets. Anyway, that's how I understand it.

A red moon starts climbing out of the plains and I try to remember if red moons have anything to do with storms and sailors taking warning. Then I remember that there aren't any sailors for about two thousand miles. One thing for sure, it ain't raining.

When I get back to the field, Harold's rig is just an unmoving black lump in the alfalfa. It jolts me because I always worry about him running over himself. This new Harold is the only hay cutter I've ever met who stops for rabbits. He gets off his tractor to move the baby ones out of the way. Getting off a tractor in the middle of the night is a sure way to kill yourself. It's too easy to bump something and start the tractor chasing you. Turn you into a farm version of an Avogadro's Number. Make a GobbleyGeek out of Harold. I drive out to see what's happened. Harold's lounging in his chair.

"What's the matter?" I ask.

"Sheared all my bolts," says Harold. "And I'm all run out of spares."

I radio Joe Bill that we need shear-bolts, then shut down the engine, and it's quiet in the alfalfa patch.

"I'm going to start a campaign to stop that baby killing," says Harold.

"It's not Christian," Harold says.

"What's going to be your slogan?" I ask.

"What?" asks Harold.

"Your saying," I say. "You gotta have a good saying or nobody'll be interested."

"Oh," says Harold, and he twists up his face to think.

I'm about to drop off.

"Let the babies keep their hearts," Harold finally says.

"That's good," I say. "You make the posters, I'll stand on street corners with you."

"If it ever rains," I say.

"Or maybe in October," I say.

This mill-hand named Randy finally shows up with the shear-bolts and I print my forehead on the steering wheel while Harold circles the field to fill his hopper. I take that load and two others, and then by my calculations I'm making my last run, which is a good thing, because on the way back to the mill I come awake twice when I'm carving up the double yellows.

It's eleven forty-five and I dump the hay and park my truck. Gus has outfoxed the coffee maker and he's standing next to Joe Bill's office door, sipping from a mug. I drag myself over to the truck barn to punch out, but before I can get there Gus starts hollering.

"Fire, we got a fire," yells Gus.

This really is almost too much already. I consider walking straight to my pickup, climbing in it, and never looking back. Only thing stopping me is that I don't know where I'd go. Smoke's already spewing through the cracks in the mill barn roof. Joe Bill comes galloping out of his office and knocks Gus flat. Then the two of them take off across the yard for the mill barn, Joe Bill looking like a bowling ball with legs, and Gus two feet taller and only legs.

This pellet mill is real prone to catching fire if you dry the hay too much. It catches in the dryer and the conveyors carry the burning through the whole building. I wander over at a safe pace. When I peek inside I see Gus flat out on his back and wondering where he's at. He's run smack into a piece of angle iron that supports one of the pellet bins. Joe Bill is cursing the fire and Gus for smacking his head. The "Number of Days Without an Accident" sign hasn't even gotten back up to half a day.

I drag Gus out of the mill and dump him on the cement pad and look at his head. He's got a square imprint between his eyes where he caught the angle iron, but there's no blood so I'm not too worried.

Back inside the mill it's a haze of pellet dust and smoke. Joe Bill has a mask over his face and a fire extinguisher in each hand and looks like a stepped-on John Wayne. He's pointing the extinguishers at the swirls of smoke and blasting away. When he breaks open the pellet press the smoke comes rolling across the floor like waves in the ocean.

"Call the fire department," yells Joe Bill.

I chug to the office but I can't find the fire department number. Then I get temporarily smarter and call the operator and she connects me.

"We got a fire at Great Western," I say.

"What's on fire?"

"Everything," I say.

Joe Bill's just inside the mill barn door, cradling an empty extinguisher. When I hear the fire engine I go drag Gus farther out of the way so he won't get run over. The firemen tear-ass into the mill and spray water all over everything and in about fifteen minutes they got it wiped out.

Gus looks at me like he might know me, but he's not sure.

"My head's noisy," says Gus.

" 'Cause you tried to knock down the mill barn with it," I say.

"Good news is it's after twelve," I say.

Joe Bill comes walking out of the mill barn. He's covered in alfalfa ashes.

"How about this idiot?" asks Joe Bill.

"He's got a headache," I say.

"You better drop him off on your way home," says Joe Bill.

"And both you better get your sleep, we're gonna have plenty catching-up cutting to do by morning," Joe Bill says.

I drag old Gus by the arm, but it's an open debate as to who should be dragging who.

Mike's sitting in his Camaro. I get Gus in the pickup and walk over to Mike.

"Say," I say to him. "You been letting Harold look at the Newsweeks?"

"Couple times," says Mike.
"You better cut that out," I say.

I pull up to Gus's trailer and honk. Gus's girlfriend comes out.
"You might want to help Gus inside," I say.
"You all right, Gus?" she asks.
"Who?" says Gus.

I take the fast road to town. Going by the sheep feedlots I hold my breath until I see two moons in the sky. I pass the gherkin factory, get visions of that poor guy glugging green-faced on the bottom of a pickle vat all those years. There's no traffic, and soon I'm winding up the canyon. Sue Ellen is probably waiting up to kick my butt for the body work I did on her car, or the body work I did on Melinda, or Melinda did on me, or either or. I think I may just let her beat me to death. The mica chips in the stones on the canyon walls catch my high beams and look like millions of little stop signs. I don't stop, I just keep driving, keep yelling, keep praying for rain.